Mystery at Marin Marsh

Denise M. Jordan
Illustrated by Carol Stutz

Rigby

Dedication

To Mrs. Knox's sixth grade advisory class at Ben Geyer Middle School:

Thank you so much for your criticisms, your suggestions, and most of all, your enthusiasm. You helped me get this project in on deadline.

Thanks also to Bill Horan, Aquatic Specialist at the Wells County Purdue University Extension office. Your expertise was invaluable.

Contents

Chapter 1

Wetlands or Wastelands?

Mrs. Knox called her sixth-grade science class to attention. "You've had time to talk. Now I need to know how each group is going to address our theme—How pollution affects our environment." She pointed to a list of topics on the chalkboard. "This list is merely a guide. If there's something else you'd like to do, and it fits our theme, just say so. I'm sure we can work something out."

Hands shot up. As Mrs. Knox called on representatives of each group, they called out their topics. She wrote names beside each topic as quickly as she could.

"Let's do waterbirds," Nezzie whispered. "You know how I love Canada geese."

"I'd rather do frogs," Tara Lynn whispered back. "They're much more interesting."

"Well, how about the food chain, then?" suggested Nezzie. "That way we could do both. What do you think, Robin?"

"I don't want to do any of it," answered Robin. She leaned forward to emphasize her words. "I hate the marsh.

It's full of bugs and weeds."

"So don't do it." Nezzie gave Robin a syrupy smile. "I'm sure Mrs. Knox will make an exception for you."

"I don't want an exception made," she snapped. "I just don't want to go into that stupid marsh." Robin paused, then asked, "Besides, why should Mrs. Knox make an exception for me?"

"Because your dad's the new art teacher," Nezzie said in a singsong voice.

"Well, he's *your* stepdad," replied Robin, "so that ought to earn you a few brownie points, too."

"Cut it out, you guys," said Tara Lynn. "You're always arguing about stupid stuff."

"Inez," said Mrs. Knox, interrupting their conversation, "what is your group's choice?"

"We want to do the marshland food chain." Nezzie looked at Tara Lynn and Robin for confirmation. Tara Lynn nodded in agreement. Robin pursed her lips and shrugged.

"The food chain," repeated Mrs. Knox as she wrote their names on the board. She continued until each group had selected a topic. Then she gave her final instructions.

"Remember, you have one week to complete this assignment. And even though the projects are group efforts, you also have individual oral reports to give. I expect each of you to explain what you gained by doing your project. Now, have a good Labor Day holiday. I'll see you all on Tuesday."

The sounds of rustling papers and murmuring voices filled the room. Then the bell rang and the students clambered to their feet.

Robin watched as Nezzie and Tara Lynn slowly made their way to the door, surrounded by a group of chattering and laughing girls. She decided to catch up, but as she got out of her seat, her foot caught on the leg of the desk. She tripped and her science book fell to the floor with a thud. Nezzie and Tara Lynn looked back.

"Come on," said Nezzie. "We've got to get the bus."

Robin stooped to pick up her book. "Dad will take us home. He said—"

"No," Nezzie interrupted. "We don't want him to take us home." She looked at Tara Lynn, then added, "At least, *I* don't."

"I don't either," agreed Tara Lynn. "I want to take the bus and find out what everyone's been doing all summer." She shifted her books to her left arm, then tucked her straight blond hair behind her ears. "Come on, let's head for our lockers and get out of here."

The three girls started down the hall. "Besides," said Nezzie, "you've got to get to know everybody, Robin. They'll think you're a geek if you have your dad take you home every day."

"All right," said Robin. "We'll take the bus."

On the bus, Nezzie and Tara Lynn joined in the noisy conversations around them. Robin watched quietly. She wondered how long it would take her to adjust to a new school and a new family situation. She sighed. Forever, probably.

Robin's parents had been divorced for two years. Robin was used to that by now. Life had actually been better after the divorce, although it meant she only saw her mother, who worked long hours as a flight attendant, every once in a while. There were no more arguments when her parents thought she was asleep. No more Mom whispering secrets into the phone. No more Dad painting dark, ugly pictures.

And she didn't really mind her dad marrying Nezzie's mother. He seemed a lot happier now. But just when she had gotten used to being a family of two, she was now part of a family of four. She wasn't sure exactly how she felt about that.

Nezzie was decent most of the time, thought Robin. It had to be hard for her, too. Nezzie's father, Dr. Jack Anderson, had died in a car accident several years ago.

Then this summer, Tom Jones—Robin's dad—had married Jill Anderson—Nezzie's mom. Everything had changed. Jill Anderson was Jill Jones. Robin had a stepmother. Nezzie had a stepfather. And the girls were instant sisters—*step*sisters.

Right after the wedding, Robin and her father had packed up their apartment in the city. They had moved to

Goose Haven Farm, where Nezzie and her mom lived. Her dad and Mama Jill had wanted to let Robin get settled into her new home before starting at a new school. A school where her father would be teaching for the first time. Robin had to admit that she liked that part.

And she liked Goose Haven Farm, too. It was a lot nicer than living in an apartment. The old farmhouse was big and rambling, with plenty of room for two more people. Robin even had her own bedroom.

Mama Jill was great, thought Robin. And she and Nezzie were working things out. Things could be worse; things could be better. She'd take it one day at a time.

But right now, she had to focus on this science project. School had hardly started and already she had work to think about. Worst of all, she was going to have to stand up and talk in front of a bunch of kids she hardly knew!

Early the next morning, someone knocked on the door at Goose Haven Farm. Robin heard Nezzie scramble down the stairs and wrench open the door. Voices floated up the stairs.

"Hey, Tara Lynn," said Nezzie.

"Hey, yourself."

"Robin's not ready yet," said Nezzie. "We gotta hurry her up."

A minute later, Robin's door burst open. "Come on, slowpoke," said Nezzie. "Tara Lynn's here."

Robin was just pulling on her shoes. "I'm ready," she said. She yawned widely as she tightened her shoelaces. "Why do we have to go so early?"

Tara Lynn laughed. "It's not that early, Robin. It's after seven. And if you want to see much in the marsh, you have to go early."

Robin flopped back on her bed and stared at the ceiling. "Well, I *don't* want to see anything. The marsh is buggy and hot and sticky." She plumped her pillow behind her head. "Wake me up when you guys get back."

Nezzie yanked the pillow away. "Get up. We've got to start on our project today."

Tara Lynn grabbed one of Robin's hands and Nezzie grabbed the other. Robin squealed as they pulled her off the bed. "OK, OK. I'm coming."

"What are you girls doing?"

They turned to see Mrs. Jones in the doorway.

"Hi, Mama," said Nezzie. "Did we wake you?"

"Hey, Mrs. J.," called Tara Lynn.

"Morning, Mama Jill," said Robin.

"Good morning," said Mrs. Jones. "I repeat, what are you girls doing?"

"We're going to Marin Marsh," answered Nezzie. "We told you and Tom last night that we were going to start on our science project today."

"Yeah," said Robin. "You and Dad gave us all those instructions about what to do and what not to do. Don't you remember?"

Mrs. Jones took off her headwrap and finger-combed her hair. "Oh, yes," she sighed. "I remember now." She covered a huge yawn with one hand. "I'm still half asleep. I heard all this thumping and bumping in here, and I just couldn't imagine—"

"Oh, Mama, I'm sorry," said Nezzie. "We didn't mean to wake you."

"It's all right," said Mrs. Jones. "I had planned to get up early anyway. I need to work on that Kwanzaa story. My editor wants it next week." She yawned again.

"You girls be careful and remember the rules." She looked sternly at Nezzie and Tara Lynn. "And take care of Robin. She didn't grow up around the marsh like you two did."

"I'm not a baby," said Robin. "I don't need them to take care of me."

"It's got nothing to do with being a baby," said Mrs. Jones. "But it has everything to do with what you are and are not familiar with. You're not familiar with the marsh, Robin. Nezzie and Tara Lynn are. If I can't trust you to follow their lead, all of you will have to wait until a grown-up can go with you."

"I'll do what they say," grumbled Robin. "But I know how to be careful." She stuck her hands in her pockets.

"Good," said Mrs. Jones. "Then I have nothing to worry about."

The girls trooped down the stairs and outside. At once, Nezzie's dog, Smitty, ran to join them. He barked and jumped up to lick Nezzie's face, his tail wagging wildly. Then he greeted Tara Lynn. The two girls giggled.

Robin backed away when she saw Smitty coming toward her, but she wasn't fast enough. Doggy breath filled her nostrils. A large, wet tongue swept her face like a slimy washcloth. Robin turned her head and pushed at the hairy beast. "Down," she cried. "Get down!"

Nezzie collared Smitty. "Sit, boy. Sit!" Smitty dropped to the ground. He looked up at Nezzie with big brown eyes, his tongue hanging lopsided out of his mouth.

"Good dog," said Nezzie as she patted him on the head. Then she looked at Robin's white blouse. It was no longer crisp and clean. The front was smeared with dirty paw marks. "Sorry," said Nezzie.

Robin brushed at the large splotches Smitty had left behind. "It'll wash," she said sadly.

"Yeah," said Tara Lynn. "It'll wash. Let's get going."

Chapter 2

Dead Fish

The girls walked toward the back boundary of the farm, Smitty trotting along beside them. About 50 feet from the house, they passed an old shed. Odd pieces of furniture and old tools littered the grass outside.

"What's all this stuff, Nez?" asked Tara Lynn.

"Tom's converting Dad's storage shed into a studio," Nezzie answered flatly.

"Yeah," chimed in Robin. "He's clearing out a lot of the junk so he can—"

"My dad's stuff is not junk!" interrupted Nezzie.

"Sorry," apologized Robin. "I didn't mean it like that. I just meant—"

"I know what you meant," snapped Nezzie.

"Besides, your mom said he could use the shed," Robin retorted. "And oil paint stinks. If he painted in the house, you'd be complaining about that."

"I know," admitted Nezzie. "But I don't like it when my dad's stuff gets thrown out so your dad can move his stuff in."

"It *will* be kind of strange to think of Dr. Jack's storage shed as an art studio," said Tara Lynn.

"Yeah," grumbled Nezzie. "It will." The girls took one last look around, then walked on, each deep in thought.

The sun was a great golden ball in the cloudless sky. The tall grass rippled in the breeze. Birdcalls filled the air with music.

"Whew," said Nezzie, "it's going to be hot today." She tucked her braids behind her ears, then wiped her brow with her hand. Her skin was starting to glisten.

"If you're hot now," asked Robin, "what are you going to be at noon? It'll be a whole lot worse then."

"You're right about that," agreed Tara Lynn. Her blond ponytail flipped from side to side as she walked. "But it'll be cooler around the water."

As the girls continued across the meadow, the terrain began to change. The ground became softer and wetter.

"Oooh," moaned Robin suddenly. Murky water covered her shoes. She backed up, muck sucking at her feet. "The ground's all wet."

Nezzie laughed. "That why they call it 'wetlands.'"

"But we're not even at the marsh yet," said Robin. "It's on the other side of the road."

"Yeah," said Nezzie, "but things start to change before you actually reach the marsh." She swept her arm wide, taking in the entire farm. "Dad said all of this used to be part of the marsh. A long time ago, people drained the land to plant crops and build houses."

Robin wiggled her toes in her wet shoes. She could

see puddles of water here and there among the tall grasses. "It doesn't look like they drained it very well."

Tara Lynn pressed a booted foot into the moist earth, then watched her footprint fill with water. "Dr. Jack used to say nature was trying to reclaim its own. He said this area was supposed to stay moist. He said it was an important ecological system."

"What's so important about wet dirt?" queried Robin. "You couldn't grow anything here. The roots would rot."

"There's plenty of stuff growing here," retorted Nezzie. "Grass and reeds and cattails."

Robin looked at the tall clumps of cattails swaying gently nearby. "What good are they?" she asked. "You can't eat them."

"Maybe *we* don't eat 'em," said Nezzie, "but other animals do." She paused, then added, "These plants give marsh creatures a safe home. You know, a habitat."

"Nezzie's right," said Tara Lynn. "In fact, I think I know why Mrs. Knox gave us this assignment. There's a bunch of people who want to drain part of the marsh to put up some condos and build a golf course. They don't think the wetlands are worth anything. I think she wants us to realize that they are."

"Draining this place seems like a good idea to me," said Robin. She looked at her damp shoes and mud-spattered legs. "Who needs squishy ground?"

"I told you to wear boots and a pair of jeans," said Nezzie.

"Why would I want to dress like that when it's 85 degrees out?" asked Robin.

"Because Mama told us to use common sense," said Nezzie.

"Well, I didn't know that meant wearing jeans and boots," said Robin. "I just thought she meant don't fall in the lake."

"That, too," Tara Lynn laughed. "Speaking of the lake, you can see it now. Look."

Robin gazed across the road at the crystal clear water that was Hominy Ridge Lake. A flock of birds was resting peacefully on the surface of the water.

Just then Smitty bounded across the road, barking a warning. The birds rose in the air in a cloud of wings and noisy honks.

Robin watched as the birds stretched out in a long line and disappeared over the woods. "They're absolutely beautiful," she marveled. "What are they?"

"Canada geese," said Nezzie. "My personal favorite."

"Geese are OK," said Tara Lynn, "but I prefer frogs." She gave a few froggy croaks.

"Oh, you and your frogs!" laughed Nezzie. "Cheer up—we ought to see plenty of them today."

The girls stopped at the hollow depression that separated Goose Haven Farm from Marin Marsh. "This ditch is filled with water," exclaimed Robin. "How are we going to get across?"

"It's not a ditch. It's called a swale," corrected Nezzie. "It's like a reservoir for the water that overflows from the creek."

"What creek?" asked Robin. "I thought it was a lake."

"There is a lake," explained Tara Lynn, "but there's a creek, too. See that bridge?"

Robin shaded her eyes with her hand and looked where Tara Lynn was pointing.

"A creek runs under that bridge and empties into the lake," explained Tara Lynn.

"Why did we come this way?" asked Robin. "Why didn't we go over the bridge instead of getting into all of this gooey stuff?"

"We will go over the bridge," said Nezzie. "But this is a shortcut to get there. It's a lot longer walk if you take the road."

A lot drier too, thought Robin.

"Do you think there are any geese nesting under the bridge?" Nezzie asked Tara Lynn as she led the way along the ditch toward the bridge.

"I doubt it," said her friend. "It's a little late in the season for that. We might find an old nest, though."

When they reached the bridge, the girls peered underneath. "No nests," said Nezzie. Carefully, she walked down the sloped bank to the water's edge. She stood there for a moment looking around. Then she inhaled deeply, breathing in the rich, moist air. "I love the smell of the water," said Nezzie. "It makes me think of coming here with Dad."

Tara Lynn followed Nezzie. She picked up a stone and threw it in the creek. It plopped loudly and sent ripples across the surface. She turned to Robin. "We always came down here with Dr. Jack," she explained. "He loved the marsh because it reminded him of where he grew up in Georgia."

Robin slowly made her way down the bank, looking for dry, solid footing. "My feet are going to be totally soaked by the time we get back," she complained. Looking around, she spied some smooth, flat rocks. She picked her way to them, then used them as stepping stones. She leaned over. The creek burbled softly and a wavery reflection stared back at her.

"I thought you said there were fish in here," said Robin. "I don't see a thing."

Nezzie laughed. "They're in there. You just have to know how to look." She squatted next to Robin and stared into the water. "See this?" Nezzie pointed to a slim gray shape. Then she touched a fingertip to the surface and the shape darted away.

"Oooh," said Robin. "I didn't even see it until it moved."

"They're camouflaged," said Tara Lynn. "Their shape and coloring keep them from being some other animal's lunch."

"What kind was it?" asked Robin. She searched the water, hoping to spot another fish. "And what kind of animal would eat it?"

"It was a bluegill," said Nezzie. "Bigger fish eat them, and some waterbirds do, too. These little guys are part of the food chain." She took her camera out of her backpack, looked around, then started snapping pictures.

Robin walked along the bank toward the lake, stepping from rock to rock. She heard Nezzie and Tara Lynn moving around, too. Their booted feet made sucking noises in the wet earth.

"Hey, I found a fish," called Robin, looking down at the water. "A dead fish."

Nezzie and Tara Lynn hurried over. A small fish floated belly-up among the tall grasses that protruded from the water.

"There's another one," said Tara Lynn. "Actually, two of them." She walked a little further down the bank. "And here's one that's still alive."

Robin and Nezzie came to look. A fish floated sideways in the murky creek. It wriggled weakly when Tara Lynn splashed it.

"This is weird," commented Nezzie. "I wonder what happened."

"What's the big deal?" asked Robin. "Fish die all the time, don't they?"

"Sure," said Nezzie, "but not so many of them at once. And you don't see them lying along the creek bank like this."

"Yeah," said Tara Lynn. "Some other animal usually eats them first."

Nezzie bent down to examine the live fish. She sniffed, wrinkling her nose like a cat. "Something smells funny." She stood and looked around. "It's coming from the lake."

"Oh, you and your nose," said Robin. "You're always saying things stink!"

"No, really," said Nezzie. "Something smells."

"This whole place smells," muttered Robin.

The girls backtracked to firmer ground. Then they climbed up onto the road. They crossed over the bridge and made their way down the trail that led to the lake.

Black and orange butterflies fluttered by, pausing occasionally on the wildflowers and shrubs that grew along the trail. Robin heard the whirring and buzzing of insect wings. She spotted a dragonfly hovering in the grass, its transparent wings gleaming like jewels in the bright sunlight.

As they got closer, Nezzie made a face.

"What's wrong?" Robin asked.

"Something really smells bad now."

"I smell it, too," admitted Robin. She wrinkled her nose and sniffed. "Kinda fishy."

"Kinda *dead* fishy," said Tara Lynn.

Just then, Smitty ran up, tail wagging wildly and fur dripping. He had a dead fish in his mouth.

"Smitty, drop it!" ordered Nezzie. She grabbed for the fish and missed. The dog danced around her, flinging raindrops of creek water from his wet fur. The fish flopped up and down as Smitty eluded Nezzie's grasp. Then he headed for Robin.

"Get away!" cried Robin as she backed up. She wanted no part of the drooling dog or the reeking fish.

Tara Lynn laughed—until Smitty turned and headed in her direction. The dog pranced around, tail wagging wildly. Then he made a wide circle and took off for the lake. Nezzie went after him.

"Get back here!" Nezzie shouted. "Bad dog!" She ran along the trail, her backpack flopping up and down. "Smitty!"

Suddenly Nezzie came to a stop. "Oh, my goodness!" she exclaimed.

She was standing frozen in place when Tara Lynn reached her. "Nezzie, what—" Tara Lynn stopped mid-sentence. "Oh no!" she said.

Robin reached the clearing where the other girls stood. Ahead of them stretched a sandy beach. But it was anything but a pleasant sight. Dead fish were everywhere. They littered the shoreline. They floated belly-up in the shallows.

Robin covered her nose and mouth to keep out the awful smell. Her stomach heaved. At last, she managed to gasp out some words. "What happened?"

"I don't know," said Nezzie. "But we're going to find out!"

Nezzie and Tara Lynn walked down to the beach and stood there. "This is crazy!" said Tara Lynn. "Fish just don't die like this."

"Something must be wrong with the water," said Nezzie. "Some kind of pollutant, maybe. I don't know what else could do this."

"Let's get out of here," called Robin from the clearing. "These dead fish are giving me the creeps."

Ignoring her stepsister, Nezzie picked up a stick and stirred the water with it.

"Come on," urged Robin. "This place reeks. I think I'm going to be sick."

"So be sick," said Nezzie. "Just do it over there." She continued to peer into the water.

Robin stepped back a few paces, hoping to get away from the smell. She paused by a tall stand of cattails, waiting impatiently for the other girls. But when she heard her name, she moved closer.

Tara Lynn was talking. "Nez, don't you think you're being a little hard on Robin?"

"Well, just listen to her!" Nezzie shot back. "Something is really wrong, and all she cares about is how bad it smells and how creepy it is. Give me a break."

"It *does* smell bad and it *is* creepy," said Tara Lynn. "Besides, this is all new to her. She's always been a city girl, remember?"

"You're right," said Nezzie. "I'm just . . . I don't know," she finished. "Sometimes, she just bugs me."

"Me, too," Tara Lynn said, "but she's not that bad, Nez."

Robin flushed angrily.

A moment later, Robin heard Nezzie call her name. "Robin? Where are you?"

"Over here," muttered Robin. Nezzie appeared around the cattails. "Look, I'm sorry, OK? But this is important. We've got to find out what happened."

Robin just nodded.

"Take a couple of slow, deep breaths," Nezzie

instructed. "That should settle your stomach. In a few minutes, you'll get used to the smell and it won't bother you so much." Nezzie grinned. "You know me and my nose. If I can get used to it, anybody can."

Robin took a long, deep breath, then slowly let it out. Then she took another breath. "Hmmm," she sighed, "I do feel better." She sniffed tentatively. "It still stinks, though."

Nezzie laughed. "Come on," she said. "We need you to help us figure out what's going on here." Together, the girls returned to the beach to join Tara Lynn.

"Look, Nezzie," said Tara Lynn. "Some fish are still alive." She pointed out several large fish moving weakly in the water and gasping for breath.

Just then, Smitty ran past them into the water, sending up a spray of smelly water. He began nosing the fish and snapping at them.

"Get out of there, Smitty," said Nezzie. "We're trying to work." The dog barked, then dashed down the shoreline.

"Did something get into the water?" asked Robin.

"I don't know what else could cause this," said Nezzie."

"Maybe it's an oil spill," said Robin. "You know, like in Alaska."

"I don't think so," said Tara Lynn. "The water doesn't look oily."

Nezzie dipped one hand in the water, then rubbed her

fingers together. "It doesn't feel oily." She sniffed her wet fingers. "It stinks. But I can't tell if it's just a dead fish smell or something else."

The girls walked down the beach, examining every nook and cranny in hopes of finding something unusual. Suddenly a flock of mallards appeared. No sooner had the ducks settled on the water than Smitty dashed toward them. The birds took flight immediately.

"Good boy, Smitty!" called Nezzie.

"I thought you didn't want him scaring off the marsh animals," commented Robin.

"Usually I don't," said Nezzie. "But think about it. If something is poisoning the water, couldn't it harm the ducks, too?

"I think we should go home and call Uncle Bill," she continued. "We've got to report this."

"Good idea," said Tara Lynn.

"Who's Uncle Bill?" asked Robin.

"He's an aquatic specialist at the county extension service," explained Nezzie. "He and my dad were fishing buddies. Uncle Bill will know what to do."

"Well, let's get out of here, then," suggested Robin. She was more than willing to leave the dead fish—and the soggy marsh—to someone else.

Chapter 3

The Investigation Begins

The girls were breathless by the time they reached the Jones's house. "What's your hurry?" asked Mrs. Jones as they rushed inside.

All three started talking at once. Nezzie's mother held up a hand and said, "Whoa! One at a time. Nezzie, tell me what's going on."

"We found a big fish kill, Mama. We need to call Uncle Bill right away."

"A fish kill! You didn't touch anything, did you?"

"No, we just looked," Nezzie assured her. "And poked at a fish with a stick."

"You stuck your hands in the water," Robin reminded her stepsister.

Mrs. Jones gave her daughter a long, hard look. "Go wash your hands," she said. "All of you. Then you can call Bill. I know he'll want to hear about this."

Two minutes later, Nezzie was dialing. Robin and Tara Lynn stood quietly, listening to one side of the conversation.

"Uncle Bill! It's me, Nezzie. Something awful has happened. There's been a fish kill.

"Yeah, yeah." Nezzie listened for a moment, then said, "It's at Marin Marsh, on the shore of Hominy Ridge Lake near the creek. There are dead and dying fish everywhere.

"No, it was me and Tara Lynn and Robin," continued Nezzie. "We were there to work on a science project and we—"

She was interrupted. "OK. I see." Her voice suddenly became more urgent. "No, Uncle Bill. I want to help you figure out what's wrong. I need to know."

Tara Lynn poked her and Nezzie corrected herself. "I mean *we* want to help," she said. She listened for a moment, then nodded and said, "OK, sure. I'll ask her."

Nezzie put one hand over the receiver. "Mama, he wants us to meet him at the bridge so we can show him where the fish kill is. But we have to have your permission."

"Let me talk to him," Mrs. Jones said. She took the phone from her daughter. "Bill, are you sure the girls won't be in the way?"

As her mother talked, Nezzie whispered to the others, "At first he just asked for directions. But I convinced him to let us come along."

"Why?" asked Robin. "Can't we just turn this over to him? After all, you said he's a specialist. And we're supposed to be researching the food chain. We've only got a week. We should go the library to do research. If we get sidetracked—"

"Don't you get it, Robin?" said Nezzie. "This *is* research. Fish are part of the food chain. If something is wrong with the fish, something could be wrong with whatever eats them."

Robin looked at Nezzie and Tara Lynn. Both girls' faces were alight with excitement. "O-O-OK," Robin dragged the word out slowly. "Then I guess I'm in, too."

Mrs. Jones hung up. "All right, girls," she said. "Bill convinced me to let you go with him. So you'd better hightail it to the bridge. He's leaving right now."

As the girls dashed out the door, Jill Jones's voice followed them. "Do exactly as he says, now!"

Ten minutes later, the girls arrived at the bridge. And not long afterward, a four-door truck pulled up. Nezzie and Tara Lynn ran to the tall, lean man who got out.

"Uncle Bill," called Nezzie. "We thought you'd never get here!"

"You're not gonna believe it," said Tara Lynn. "I've never seen so many dead fish."

The man took his cap off, scratched his head, then settled the cap back in place. "How you girls doin'?" he asked in a slow drawl. He put his arms around their shoulders and walked with them toward Robin.

"You must be Robin," he said. "I'm Bill Harris. I met your dad a couple of weeks ago." He shook Robin's hand, then nodded in Tara Lynn and Nezzie's direction. "These two call me Uncle Bill. We go way back. I taught 'em all they know about fishing. You can call me Uncle Bill, too, if you like. And if that doesn't work, call me Bill or Mr. Harris. Doesn't matter to me."

Robin grinned. This tall, slow-talking man reminded her of her grandfather. Bill Harris was years younger, but he had the same old-fashioned mannerisms and southern drawl. She felt instantly comfortable with him. "Uncle Bill will be fine, sir."

"No need to 'sir' me," he said. He turned to include Nezzie and Tara Lynn. "OK, let's get this show on the road. Tell me what's happened."

The girls filled him in, starting with the dead fish in the creek and ending with the fish kill on the beach. He listened intently until they were finished.

"All right. Get in the truck and we'll drive down there," said Uncle Bill. "Once I see the kill, I might have a better idea of what's going on."

The girls climbed in the backseat and put on their seat belts. Uncle Bill started the engine, and they bumped over the rough road to Hominy Ridge Lake.

"Yep," drawled Uncle Bill as they approached the

beach, "it smells pretty ripe."

At the site of the fish kill, he walked up and down and back and forth, studying the scene without speaking.

"Looks like somethin' awful bad happened 'round here," said Uncle Bill at last. "I wonder what it was." He nudged a large fish with the toe of his boot. Then he knelt on the shore and looked at the fish tangled and floating in the grasses.

He rose to his feet. "Yep, good thing you called me, girls. You sure did stumble over a mess here. The question is, do we have some kind of disease or some kind of toxin?"

"How can you tell the difference?" asked Robin.

"There are ways," said Uncle Bill. "Come on. You girls can help." He strode away from the lake with all three girls behind him.

At the truck, Uncle Bill lifted the tailgate and started removing supplies. "We'll do this the scientific way," he said. He handed out disposable gloves, saying, "Put these on. They'll be too big, but they'll do the job."

The girls pulled on the gloves while Uncle Bill lifted a large box and a cooler from the truck. He set both on the ground.

"Why'd you bring a cooler?" asked Tara Lynn.

"We gotta keep our specimens cold until we get 'em to the lab," said Uncle Bill.

"What lab?" asked Nezzie.

"We'll take them to Sarah," said Uncle Bill as he continued to rummage in the back of his truck.

"Take these," he continued, handing Robin several nets. Then he lifted out a video camera and headed back toward the lake.

"Who's Sarah?" asked Robin as she ran to keep up.

"She runs a small biology lab in town," explained Uncle Bill. "I often call her in on cases like this."

He turned on the camera, focused the lens, then began talking as he videotaped the shoreline. He identified himself, gave the date, the time, and the location. He even described the weather conditions.

"Hundreds of fish appear to be washed up here on the beach," said Uncle Bill, still talking and taping. "Large and small fish of a number of species are included in the die-off. I see bass, bluefish, and catfish." He paused, then added, "The fish that are still alive are listless with inconsistent swimming motions. There is some flashing, but no piping can be observed."

"What does he mean?" whispered Robin. "What's flashing and piping?"

"Look there." Nezzie pointed to several fish. "See how they're kind of flopping back and forth?"

Robin saw several large fish swimming sideways. They struggled to right themselves, exposing their lighter underbellies as they wriggled about.

"That's flashing," explained Nezzie.

"And piping is when the fish come up to the top and try to breathe," Tara Lynn added. "They look like they're sucking air."

"Oh," said Robin.

Uncle Bill interrupted his taping to call out, "Nezzie, bring me that big catfish over there."

Robin watched as Nezzie lifted the large fish with her gloved hands.

"Stretch it out flat on the ground," Uncle Bill instructed. He videotaped the fish from one side, then asked Nezzie to turn it over. At the same time, he continued to record his observations. "No obvious open sores," he said. "Gills are flaring and discolored, eyes bulging.

"OK, Nezzie, you can put that fish back. But we need to get shots of some small ones."

The girls followed as he walked along the beach, taping fish and describing what he saw. Finally he shut the camera off. "That's enough video," he said. "Let's collect some samples."

He started back toward the box he had removed from the truck. "Come on, girls. You can help. But first we'll need some supplies." He rooted through the box, then handed each girl an amber quart-size jar.

"Are we gonna put the fish in here?" asked Nezzie.

"No," said Uncle Bill. "I've got some aluminum foil

for that. These are for taking water samples."

They trooped down to the lake. "Rinse the jars out first," instructed Uncle Bill, "then fill 'em up."

Robin watched as Uncle Bill took the lid off and swished it around in the water. He did the same thing with the jar. Next, he filled the jar with water and screwed the lid back on.

She copied his actions carefully, as did Nezzie and Tara Lynn. Then they followed Uncle Bill back up the bank. He took the lid off the cooler and showed them how to put the jars inside so the ice surrounded them.

"What do we do now?" asked Robin.

"Now we're going to collect some dead fish and get out of here," said Uncle Bill. "The warmer it gets, the worse it's going to smell."

"Should we pick up the fish on the beach?" asked Tara Lynn.

"No," said Uncle Bill, "we'll net some that are still in the water. That way we don't contaminate 'em any more than they already are." He eyed Robin's sneaker-clad feet. "Since you aren't wearing boots, you'd better help me wrap fish, Robin."

Holding a net in one hand, he waded into the lake until the water almost reached the top of his tall boots. Then he dipped the net beneath the surface, under a floating fish. When he pulled the net out of the water, the fish was inside.

As he came back to the shore, he said, "See how easy it is? Nezzie and Tara Lynn, you can net more samples. Then bring them to Robin and me."

Uncle Bill ripped off a sheet of aluminum foil. He wrapped it around the fish he had netted. "The shiny side goes out," he explained to Robin.

"Why?"

"Because the other side hasn't been exposed to the air. So there is less chance of adding anything foreign to the specimen."

He handed the wrapped fish to Robin. "You can pack our samples in the ice cooler. That will preserve them until we get them to Sarah."

Robin looked uneasily at the foil-wrapped parcel. Yuck, she thought. Thank goodness for gloves!

They all worked steadily. Nezzie and Tara Lynn splashed in the water, netting fish and getting wet. Uncle Bill wrapped the samples. And Robin packed them in the cooler full of ice.

She was squatting by the cooler, depositing yet another fish, when Smitty appeared from nowhere. He ran up and sniffed at the foil packet in her hands. Then he stuck his cold, wet nose in her face.

"Ugh!" cried Robin, pushing the dog away. She lost her balance and toppled backward. Wet earth made contact with the back of her legs and soaked through her shorts.

Smitty!" yelled Robin. "Get away!"

Giving her a hurt look, the dog ran off down the beach. As Robin struggled to her feet, she saw that Tara Lynn and Nezzie were doubled over with laughter. Even Uncle Bill was chuckling.

"It's not funny," protested Robin. She brushed at the mud and sand on her legs and shorts. "How would you like it if that stupid dog jumped all over you?" she asked angrily.

No one answered. They just kept laughing.

Robin stared at the three of them for several minutes. Finally, she began to laugh, too.

"OK, girls," said Uncle Bill at last, "let's pack it in. I think we've got enough." He gave another chuckle, then added, "I know some of us have certainly had enough."

Uncle Bill lugged the heavy cooler back up to the truck. The girls brought the rest of the equipment. Then they all climbed in.

"Do you suppose he's going to take us all home now?" whispered Nezzie.

"Take you home?" echoed Uncle Bill, who had heard her. "Why would I do that? You girls discovered this mystery. So, in my book, that means you get to come along to see if Sarah can help to solve it."

As he started the engine, Nezzie and Tara Lynn exchanged a satisfied look. Robin stared out the window, thinking about dry shoes and clean clothes. She wasn't entirely sure how happy she was about being part of this detective team.

Chapter 4

A Mountain of Clues

Fifteen minutes later, Uncle Bill turned the truck into the parking lot of a small brick building. A sign outside read "Biology Laboratory, Fort Wayne, IN, Sarah Rosario, Ph.D."

"Well, let's see if anyone's here," Uncle Bill said.

"It's Saturday," said Robin. "Would she be working?"

"Knowing Sarah, I'd say there's a good chance of that," replied Uncle Bill. "She spends more time here than she does at home."

They got out of the truck and walked up to the door. Nezzie rang the bell. When no one answered immediately, she rang again.

"Hold your horses," drawled Uncle Bill. "Give the woman time to get to the door. She's probably alone out in the lab."

"Sorry," said Nezzie. "I just can't wait for—"

She was interrupted by the opening of the door. A tall young woman with curly brown hair stood there. "Hello!

This is an unexpected pleasure!" she exclaimed. Then she reached out to hug Nezzie and Tara Lynn.

As the woman turned to smile at Robin, Smitty charged forward. "Down, boy!" Sarah commanded. To Robin's surprise, the dog obeyed.

Sarah stepped back and motioned everyone inside— even Smitty. "What are you guys doing here?" she asked.

"We found a big fish kill," said Nezzie.

"At Marin Marsh," added Tara Lynn.

"It stunk," said Robin. "Even the water smelled." Then something occurred to her for the first time. "Nezzie," she said, "what about Smitty? Is that water going to make him sick, too? I mean, he was in the water. And the fish are dying. And—"

At Nezzie's look of horror, Robin stopped talking. She wished she hadn't said anything.

"I didn't even think about that," moaned Nezzie, grabbing Smitty and pulling him to her. "Oh, I hope he's OK!"

"OK, everybody. Let's calm down," said Uncle Bill. "Sarah, I don't think we need to worry about Smitty, do you? He was running around in the water, but I didn't see him drinking it. And even if he did, he couldn't have had enough to cause any harm."

"Don't panic, Nezzie. He should be fine," said Sarah. "Now, tell me about this fish kill. What do you think caused it?"

"I don't have a clue," admitted Uncle Bill. "But the girls helped me collect some samples. We've got them out in the truck."

"Well, bring them in!" said Sarah. "I'll take a look right now."

The girls waited with Sarah while Uncle Bill went back to the truck to get the cooler.

"We weren't sure you would be here," said Nezzie.

"But we kinda thought you might be since you're here so much," said Tara Lynn.

"I'm here," said Sarah. "I've got a special project that I'm working on this weekend." She looked at Robin. "So who are you?"

"I'm Robin, Nezzie's stepsister."

"Hi, Robin. I'm Sarah Rosario." She stuck out her hand. "It's so nice to meet you." Robin smiled as they shook hands.

Just then Uncle Bill arrived with the cooler. He thumped it down on the counter, then removed a few wrapped fish.

"We collected a variety of samples," he said. "We wanted to give you as much to work with as possible."

Sarah put on disposable gloves and opened one of the packets. "Hmmm," she said as she turned the fish over and examined it carefully. The girls crowded around the table and watched silently.

"I don't see any signs of disease," Sarah said. Then she

reached for another foil-wrapped packet. "Are they all like this?" she asked.

"Yes," said Uncle Bill. "No open sores or anything like that on them. Nothing that we could see."

"Tell me about the water," Sarah instructed. As Uncle Bill began to talk, she moved about the lab collecting pieces of equipment.

He proceeded to tell her his impressions of the water and the plants that grew in it and nearby. He finished by saying, "I think there's some kind of toxin in the water."

Taking a scalpel, Sarah sliced the fish open. Robin's eyes widened and her dark skin paled when she saw the pink, gray, and red innards spill onto the table. She gagged.

Sarah neatly pulled away the yellowish bag of fish eggs and put them aside. She continued her dissection, examining one organ, then another.

Robin stared at the slimy, gooey mass of fish eggs and innards. She stepped back from the table and took several slow, deep breaths. Her eyes went to Nezzie and Tara Lynn. They hadn't noticed her reaction. They were both watching Sarah intently and asking questions.

Nothing seems to bother them, thought Robin. Taking another deep breath to settle her stomach, she moved back to the table. I can do this, she told herself. I am not a wimp. I am not going to faint. I can do this, she repeated silently.

"Well," said Sarah a few minutes later, "based on this examination, I don't see any signs of disease. So I agree with you, it's probably some kind of toxin. Something is in the water." She paused and pushed her glasses to the top of her head. "You'll need to get that water analyzed."

"I know," said Uncle Bill, "but the environmental lab's closed for the holiday. I'll have to keep the water samples refrigerated until it opens."

"I won't have anything more to tell you until I run some tests anyway," said Sarah. She looked at the girls' eager faces. "Don't worry. I'll call Bill as soon as I know anything."

"OK," said Uncle Bill. "In the meantime, I'll take these girls home and make some phone calls."

They said their good-byes and piled into the truck. All the way home, the girls bombarded Uncle Bill with questions. However, he had no answers. "We'll have to wait and see," he said more than once.

He pulled into the driveway at Goose Haven Farm. As the girls jumped out of the truck, the door to the house opened, and Nezzie's mother and Robin's father stepped onto the porch.

"Bill," Mrs. Jones called, "what did you find out?"

"Not much," said Uncle Bill. "I took some fish samples over to Sarah Rosario's office. She'll run some tests, then let me know. I've got some water samples to take to the lab, but I can't do that until Tuesday." He smiled regretfully. "Sometimes, these long holiday weekends are a pain in the neck."

Mr. Jones chuckled. "You'd have a hard time convincing *me* of that, Bill." He put his arm around Robin's shoulder and pulled her close to him. "So what do we do in the meantime?"

"Nothing. We've done all we can for now." Uncle Bill got into his truck, fastened his seat belt, and started the engine. "As soon as I know something, I'll call you." He backed out and drove off.

"OK," said Mr. Jones, "while we eat lunch, you can tell us about this discovery you made in the marsh."

They trooped into the kitchen. As they ate, the girls told their story. When they had finished, Mr. Jones said, "I think I'd like to check things out for myself. This whole thing worries me, especially since the creek is so close to the farm."

"I want to look around some more, too," said Nezzie. "Why don't we go back this afternoon?"

"Dad, it's kind of smelly out there—" began Robin.

"You don't have to come," interrupted Nezzie. "You can stay here with Mama. Tara Lynn and I can—"

"I didn't say I wasn't coming," said Robin hotly. "I was just trying to warn Dad about what to expect. If you're going, I'm going."

"Count me in, too," said Tara Lynn. "I'll just call home and let Mom know what's up."

"That's a good idea," said Mrs. Jones. "Let me speak to her before you hang up." She poured herself a glass of lemonade. "And I'm coming, too. You're not leaving me out. I'm just as concerned about the marsh as you are."

Later that afternoon, the girls retraced their steps to the lake. Mr. and Mrs. Jones walked behind them.

Long before they got to the water, the smell of dead fish reached them. "Whew!" said Tom. "You were right, Robin. It is pretty ripe."

"Just take deep breaths, Dad," said Robin. "You'll get used to it." She glanced at Nezzie and grinned.

At the beach, Mr. and Mrs. Jones studied the scene with horror. "Man," said Robin's father, "what a mess!"

"Who's going to clean it up?" asked Robin.

"I don't know," said Mrs. Jones. She stepped carefully across the fish-littered beach. "I don't think they'll start the clean-up until they determine the cause of the fish kill," she said. "They have to know what they're dealing with so they know how to dispose of the dead fish."

Robin stayed close to her father and stepmother while Nezzie and Tara Lynn walked on ahead. She showed them where they had collected the fish samples. She sheepishly pointed out where Smitty had knocked her down.

"Mama, Tom," called Nezzie, "we're gonna follow the creek for a bit. We want to see if there's anything else up there."

"Go ahead," said Mrs. Jones. "We're right behind

you." She picked her way along the path. "But if you find any other signs of trouble, you call us."

"OK," said Nezzie.

"Wait for me," called Robin. She ran to catch up with Nezzie and Tara Lynn.

The three girls chattered as they walked along the rough bank. They had gone about half a mile when Nezzie came to a sudden halt.

"What's that?" she asked.

"What's what?" replied Tara Lynn.

"Where?" asked Robin.

"That," said Nezzie. "Up there. See where the creek curves around into those trees?"

Robin squinted. "You're right. There *is* something there, but I don't know what it is."

"Come on," said Nezzie. She started to walk faster.

"Shouldn't we wait for Mama Jill and Dad?" asked Robin.

"You wait if you want to," said Tara Lynn. "We're going to look."

The girls hurried along the creek bank. As they got closer, Tara Lynn said, "Whatever it is, it sure does stink!"

"There's definitely something there," added Robin. "We should—"

Nezzie didn't wait for Robin to finish. She turned around and yelled, "Hey, Mama and Tom! There's something up here. You guys better come and see."

Mr. and Mrs. Jones picked up their pace, soon catching up with the girls. Before long, Robin could see the mound clearly.

"Yuck! It's garbage!" she cried.

A huge pile of trash and junk started at the edge of an access road. It tumbled down a slight slope and into the creek. Some debris floated near the bank.

"Where in the world did this come from?" asked Mrs. Jones as she stared at the trash heap.

"Somebody's been illegally dumping," said Tom. "They have to know that it's against the law. There are signs all over that say so."

"I wonder how long this garbage has been here," said Mrs. Jones.

"We were here just a month ago, Mama," said Nezzie. "We came out for a picnic and a hike. Remember?"

"I remember," said her mother. "It was beautiful. There was certainly no trash here then."

"So who dumped it?" asked Nezzie. "And when did they do it?"

"And why?" added Robin. "Why would anyone do such a disgusting thing?"

Chapter 5

Camping Out

"Since when did you care so much about the environment?" Nezzie asked Robin. She moved closer to the heap and kicked at an empty food can.

"I've always cared," said Robin. "Just because I don't like the marsh doesn't mean I don't care about nature."

Ignoring them, Tara Lynn bent to pick something up.

"Don't touch anything!" said Mr. Jones sharply.

"It's just a piece of paper," protested Tara Lynn. "I think it's a letter. There's a name or something on it. Maybe we could—"

"No," said Mr. Jones, "I don't want you girls to touch anything. Who knows what's in this mess." He walked around the trash pile. "There's all kinds of junk in here. Some stuff could be dangerous. Come on. We're heading back to the house to call Uncle Bill and let him know what we found."

A short time later, Robin's father was on the phone. He told Bill Harris about finding the dump site and described some of the debris they had seen.

"Yes," said Mr. Jones into the phone, "I agree." He swiveled in his chair and leaned his elbow on the desk.

"I'd like to find the guilty parties, too. OK, I'll expect to hear from you."

"What did he say?" asked Robin as soon as her father had hung up.

"He was upset, but he wasn't real surprised. He's going to notify the proper authorities and get back to us," said Tom.

"What does that mean?" asked Nezzie. "Who're the proper authorities?"

"I don't know," said Mr. Jones. "Probably the DNR— the Department of Natural Resources. Bill knows who to contact. Let's let him do his job. He said he'd call as soon as he had something to tell us."

"Oh, all right," said Nezzie. She plopped down on the floor near her mother. "But I hope it doesn't take too long. I can't stand the thought that somebody is ruining our marsh by dumping garbage out there."

"Me either," said Tara Lynn. "I just can't imagine how anybody could do a thing like this."

"What I still don't understand is *why*," said Robin. "There are plenty of landfills and junkyards. Why don't they just take the stuff there?"

"Greed," said Mrs. Jones. "Some people don't want to pay the fees that landfills and junkyards charge to dispose of refuse properly." She fingered Nezzie's braids thoughtfully. "Hopefully the authorities will find out who did this and put a stop to it." Then she stood up and stretched. "In the meantime, I've got an article to finish. I'll talk to all of you later." She headed for her office—a small room at the back of the house.

The girls gathered upstairs in Nezzie's room to discuss the situation. Robin and Tara Lynn made themselves comfortable on Nezzie's bed. Nezzie paced back and forth.

"Sarah thinks something probably got into the water," said Nezzie. "Now we know how."

"You're jumping to conclusions," said Robin. "Just because all that stuff was dumped out there doesn't mean that's the cause of the fish kill."

"It's got to be," said Nezzie indignantly. "What else could have caused it?"

"Well, it makes sense," said Tara Lynn. "Something from that dump site is probably contaminating the water." She sighed deeply. "But we can't be sure. Not 'til we get the results of the fish testing and the water analysis."

"Exactly," said Robin. "That's what I meant. Nezzie's probably right, but we can't be sure. And," she paused for emphasis, "there's nothing we can do about that. What I want to know is who put that stuff out there."

"I'd like to know that, too," said Nezzie. She stopped pacing and stared at the other two girls. "Got any ideas?"

"Hey," said Tara Lynn, "I saw a battered old truck going down the access road toward the marsh yesterday." She sat up and swung her legs over the side of the bed.

"Mom and I were going to the store. I just happened to notice it because it was an odd shade of yellow. And because you don't see many trucks on that road."

"You think they were dumping a load of trash?" asked Robin.

"I don't know," said Tara Lynn. "Maybe."

"Hmmm," said Nezzie. "I saw a beat-up yellow truck the other day, too. It was parked somewhere, though." She paused, brows furrowed, lips pursed. Then she snapped her fingers. "I remember. It was at the Fosters' place." She turned to Robin. "You know Roger Foster, right? He's in our class at school."

"I don't think Roger's dad has a yellow truck," said Tara Lynn. "I heard some kids calling Mr. Foster's truck the Dustmobile. Roger said it was hard to keep a black truck from looking dusty when you live on a dirt road."

"Well, maybe the truck doesn't belong to the Fosters," said Robin. "But Tara Lynn saw a yellow truck headed for the marsh. And Nezzie saw a yellow truck in Roger's driveway. So we should find out who it belongs to and what it's being used for."

"And how do we do that?" asked Nezzie.

"Why don't we just call and ask?" suggested Robin.

"Oh, sure. And if Roger's dad has been illegally dumping garbage in the marsh, he'll just tell us."

"No," said Robin, "we'd have to be careful how we ask. We have to think like detectives if we want to find out what's going on."

"Detectives, huh?" said Nezzie. "You read too many mysteries, Robin."

"Wait, Nez," said Tara Lynn. "Robin's got a point."

"Fine," said Nezzie. "Who's going to call?"

"I will," said Robin.

"What are you going to say?" asked Tara Lynn.

"I don't know," said Robin, "but I'll think of something." She got up and headed for the door. Nezzie and Tara Lynn started to follow. "You guys stay here," she ordered. "You'll just make me nervous. I'll let you know what I find out."

"OK," said Nezzie. "We'll wait."

"But you better tell us everything," said Tara Lynn.

Robin grinned. "I will. Just hold your horses," she drawled in a good imitation of Uncle Bill.

She was back a short time later. "Looks like a dead end," she sighed. "The truck belongs to Roger's grandfather, who's visiting this weekend. They were fishing. That's probably when you saw the truck."

"Fishing," said Nezzie skeptically. "How do you know Roger didn't make that up? You didn't just ask him if he went to the marsh in a yellow truck, did you?"

"Of course not," said Robin. "I made up this story about a scavenger hunt and looking for yellow things. Then I brought up the truck business. It's not them, I tell you."

Tara Lynn sighed heavily. "You're right. Roger's

grandfather lives hours away, at the other end of the state. If he just came for the weekend, he didn't do the dumping. That stuff has been there for more than a few days."

Nezzie gave in. "OK, it was worth a try. At least we can rule the yellow truck out. On to Plan B." She looked at Robin and Tara Lynn. "What *is* Plan B?"

"What if we could catch someone in the act?" asked Tara Lynn.

"How?" asked Robin.

"We could camp out and wait for someone to show up with a load of trash."

"Now *that's* a good idea, Tara Lynn," said Nezzie.

"Yeah, but do we want to be there when somebody's illegally dumping? Besides, I don't think Dad and Mama Jill will go for this idea," said Robin.

"Tara Lynn and I camp out all the time during the summer," said Nezzie. "Mama will say yes, I know it. I'll go ask."

Five minutes later, she was back. "Start packing," she said. "We're going camping."

"I'll be back with my stuff in 15 minutes," promised Tara Lynn.

Robin wasn't sure she wanted to spend the night outside, but she certainly wasn't going to admit that to Nezzie. So she pulled her sleeping bag out of the closet. Then she changed into long pants. She wasn't going to make that mistake again.

By the time Nezzie and Robin lugged their things downstairs and onto the porch, Tara Lynn was already there. She was down on one knee, scratching Smitty behind the ears.

Mr. and Mrs. Jones came out to say good-bye. "Do you have everything, Nezzie?" asked her mother.

"We just need to get the tent from the garage."

"I don't know," said Robin. "It seems to me that we ought to need more than a flashlight, water, cookies, and fruit."

"Robin," said Nezzie, "if we need anything else, we're close enough to come back and get it."

"I guess," said Robin. "I'm just a little nervous. I've never been camping before."

"Then it's high time you went," said Mrs. Jones. "You'll enjoy it. Nezzie's dad fixed a site out in the meadow when the girls were little. It's close enough to be safe, but far enough away so you'll feel like you're on your own."

She leaned over to ruffle Smitty's fur. "Besides, Smitty will be with you. Nothing's going to come close with him around."

"That makes me feel better," said Mr. Jones. "I'm not real sure about letting them camp out by themselves, Jill."

"Tom," said Mrs. Jones, "it's perfectly safe. They'll be in our backyard."

Robin looked at Nezzie. Wasn't the whole point of camping out to watch the dump site? Could they even see it from the meadow?

Before Robin could ask any questions, Nezzie spoke up. "We'll be fine, Tom," she said. "Just fine."

"All right," he replied. "Have fun, girls, and we'll see you in the morning."

The girls picked up their camping supplies and started down the driveway toward the garage. They stopped long enough for Nezzie to get the small tent. She put the carrying bag over one shoulder and handed her sleeping bag to Tara Lynn to carry.

As soon as they were out of hearing distance, Robin said, "Nezzie, I'm not sure about this. Dad thinks we're going to be camping out in the meadow. We're not, are we?"

"You can stay in the meadow if you want," said Nezzie. "But I'm not going to. And neither is Tara Lynn. Camping near the dump site is the only way to see what's going on out there. If they knew where we were really going, they'd never let us go. So we just aren't telling them."

"If my mom finds out," said Tara Lynn, "I'll be grounded for life."

"All of us will," said Nezzie, "but it's for a good cause. We'll just have to make sure they don't find out."

They trudged on without talking. Robin wasn't sure how she felt. She didn't like misleading her father. But she certainly didn't want Nezzie to think she was afraid of camping near the dump site. Even if she was.

Tara Lynn broke the silence. "Where should we set up camp?" she asked.

"I've been thinking about that," said Nezzie. "We want to get close enough to see the dump site, but not close enough for anybody to see us."

"We have to make sure we're not near the lake," said Robin. "Mama Jill would have a fit."

"I'm not dumb, Robin," said Nezzie. "I know better than to mess around near water in the dark. But I was thinking, if we camped in that grove of trees . . . You know, Tara, the place where we found those arrowheads last summer?"

"That would be perfect!" cried Tara Lynn.

"If we camped there," continued Nezzie, "we could use my binoculars to spy on the dump site."

"And the ground's pretty firm over there," said Tara Lynn. "We shouldn't have to worry about wet spots."

"It does sound good," said Robin, "if you're sure we can't be seen."

"I'm sure," said Nezzie. "The access road is the only way a truck could get to the dump site. We won't be camped close to the road, but we'll be able to hear if anyone comes. And with the binoculars, we'll be able to see them, but they won't be able to see us."

Their campsite settled upon, the girls picked up their pace. By the time the sky began to darken, the tent was up. Soon afterward, they were in their sleeping bags.

Robin could hear Smitty snuffling around outside the

tent. She also heard other less-familiar noises. Cicadas hummed and owls hooted in the distance. Small animals rustled in the grass, and the wind ruffled the leaves of the trees. She scooted her sleeping bag closer to Nezzie and Tara Lynn.

The girls lay in the tent like caterpillars wrapped in cocoons. They talked into the night, whispering so they would hear any vehicles that approached the dump site. They talked and they listened and they waited. Robin's eyelids drooped as it got later and later.

Smitty's barking woke her.

"Someone's out there!" cried Robin.

"It's the dumpers!" said Tara Lynn excitedly.

Nezzie scrambled out of her sleeping bag and peered outside. "What is it, Smitty?" she asked in a hoarse whisper. She crawled out of the tent. Tara Lynn and Robin tumbled out after her.

Nezzie hurried to Smitty, who was barking wildly and trying to climb a tree.

"Where are the binoculars?" asked Tara Lynn.

"Here," said Robin. "I fell asleep with them around my neck." She put the binoculars up to her eyes and focused on the dump site. "I don't see anything."

"Let me try," demanded Tara Lynn. She snatched the binoculars and zeroed in on the area. "You're right. There's nothing there. So what's up with Smitty? Why all the ruckus?"

"He must be after something," said Robin. Carrying

their flashlights, she and
Tara Lynn hurried over to
Nezzie and Smitty. The dog
was still barking and throwing himself against the trunk of the tree.

"What is it?" asked Robin. "What's
he so upset about?"

"I think it's a raccoon," said Nezzie.
"Look up there."

Tara Lynn and Robin stared into the
branches overhead. A pair of eyes, gleaming like
pearls, looked down on them. Tara Lynn's flashlight
clearly outlined the shape of a large raccoon.

"That dumb dog scared me to death," said Robin.

Nezzie gripped Smitty's collar and dragged him away from the tree. As she struggled with the dog, she tripped over something. Smitty escaped and rushed back to renew his attack on the tree.

"Look at this," said Nezzie.

"My backpack!" said Tara Lynn. "That raccoon stole it right out of the tent!"

"It was after the food," said Robin as she scanned the area with her flashlight. Cookies and half-eaten apple slices littered the ground. "How did it get into the tent without being noticed?"

"Some detectives we turned out to be," said Nezzie in disgust. "We couldn't even hear a raccoon when it was practically on top of us."

By the time the girls had picked up the mess, Smitty had given up. Girls and dog settled down inside the tent.

"OK, we have to keep each other awake all night," ordered Nezzie.

"Pretend it's a pajama party," yawned Tara Lynn.

"Yeah," said Robin. "No one ever sleeps at those."

However, the next thing Robin knew, the morning sun was teasing her eyelids. "Hey, guys, the night's over," she cried, shaking Nezzie and Tara Lynn awake.

The girls stumbled out of the tent, stretching and yawning. A quick check with the binoculars revealed no sign of new dumping.

"A whole night wasted," said Nezzie wearily.

"Yeah," agreed Robin. "Let's go home and get some sleep."

Chapter 6

Plan C

The girls stowed the tent in the shed. Then they walked back to the house. But instead of going inside, they sat on the porch steps to talk.

"What a waste of time," said Nezzie. "We spent the whole night out there and didn't learn a thing."

Tara Lynn scratched at a mosquito bite. "I wonder when Uncle Bill or Sarah will know something."

"Not before Tuesday, that's for sure," said Robin. "Today is Sunday, and tomorrow is Labor Day."

"Right," said Nezzie, "so on to Plan C."

"I didn't know we had a Plan C," said Robin. "What is it?"

"I'm working on it," said Nezzie.

"Hey," said Tara Lynn, "remember when we were at the dump site with Tom and Mrs. J.?"

"Yeah," replied Nezzie and Robin in one voice.

"Well, remember that I was looking at a letter and Tom told me not to touch it?"

"Yeah," Robin and Nezzie said again.

"Maybe we could go back and find it."

"How would that help?" asked Robin.

"It could give us a clue about the person who is doing the illegal dumping," said Tara Lynn.

"It wouldn't be much of a clue," said Nezzie. "What would—"

"Wait a minute," interrupted Robin. "Tara Lynn might be right. The letter might have a name or address or something that tells us who the garbage belongs to."

"And?" prompted Nezzie.

"And if we find out who the trash belongs to, maybe we can find out who dumped it there."

"Good thinking, guys," said Nezzie. "It just might work."

"Well, we can't go back now," said Tara Lynn, glancing at her watch. "I have to head home before they send the troops out to find me."

"And we have to go to the community pancake breakfast," said Nezzie. "So let's all meet here after lunch, OK? To discuss Plan C."

"Whatever that is," laughed Robin.

On the way home from breakfast, Robin nudged Nezzie, who was sitting beside her on the backseat. "When are you going to ask them?" she whispered.

"Soon," Nezzie whispered back. She smoothed the skirt of her dress and stared out the car window.

Robin sighed and sat back. She and Nezzie had come up with Plan C while they dressed. Robin had held firm on one thing. "We have to tell Dad and Mama Jill what we're doing," she had insisted. "I don't want to spend the rest of my life grounded."

Nezzie had agreed. But so far, she hadn't brought up the subject of returning to the marsh.

Now, at last, Nezzie said softly, "Mama?"

"Hmmm," murmured Mrs. Jones. She rested in the seat with her head back and her eyes closed.

"I was just thinking . . . "

When Nezzie didn't finish, her mother opened her eyes and turned to look behind her. "What were you thinking, Nezzie?"

"Well, I was thinking about what's going on in the marsh."

"So was I," added Robin quickly.

Nezzie continued. "Yeah, see, we've been learning in school all about how we have to be good caretakers of the environment. And it sure seems like whoever is doing the dumping is anything but a good caretaker."

"I'd have to agree with you there, honey," said Mrs. Jones. "It's an awful thing to do."

There was a moment of silence; then Robin nudged Nezzie again.

"So Robin and I were kind of wondering about checking out the dump site again," said Nezzie. "We thought that if we looked through some of the stuff, we could sort of figure out who's doing it."

"Yeah," agreed Robin as she played nervously with her hair. "We thought we could find some kind of clues."

"Absolutely not!" said Mr. Jones. "Do you know how dangerous mucking around in that trash could be?"

"But, Dad," began Robin.

"No 'buts'," he said. "Let Uncle Bill and the authorities handle it. You girls have done enough."

"Tom," said Mrs. Jones, "let's not be too quick to say no."

"Are you out of your mind, Jill?" said Mr. Jones hotly. "Do you seriously think—"

Robin tensed, wondering if her father and Mama Jill were going to have a big argument.

But Nezzie's mother just said calmly, "Let me tell you some things that you don't know, OK? Then we can make a decision." She looked at him squarely. "After all, Tom, it wouldn't be like you to jump to conclusions without having all the facts."

"Well, what facts don't I have?" Robin's father glanced at his wife, then turned his attention back to the road.

"A few years ago, there was a cleanup at Reservoir Park. The park had gotten really polluted. People were dumping things there and the fish were dying. So the city decided to clean it up. They asked for volunteers, and Jack and I took Nezzie and Tara Lynn along with us."

"So?" asked Mr. Jones.

"So the girls learned that when something threatens the environment, you do something about it."

She paused to make sure she had his attention. "Really, it was quite safe. They wore jeans, long-sleeved shirts, boots, and gloves. The whole event was carefully supervised and there were specific guidelines."

She turned to look at her daughter. "When you consider the way Nezzie and Robin have been raised, it makes sense for them to want to find out who's responsible. I think if they just look around the edges of the dump site, it would be safe enough."

Before her husband could protest, she continued, "Not by themselves, of course. We'll go with them again."

Robin leaned toward the front seat, wondering what her father would say.

"Well, what exactly are you girls looking for?" he asked.

"Tara Lynn saw a letter, Dad," said Robin. "We were thinking that if we could find names or addresses on some of the junk, we'd have something to go on."

"Right," said Nezzie. "The letter Tara Lynn saw was right out in the open. We wouldn't have to dig through the trash. And we could wear gloves, just like we did when we cleaned up the reservoir."

"Who do you think you are, Nancy Drew?" asked Mr. Jones.

Nezzie looked blank. "Who's Nancy Drew?"

"Some girl detective," explained Robin. "My mom has a whole set of Nancy Drew books that she saved for me from when she was a girl."

Robin reached out to touch her father's shoulder. "Dad, we just want to look around. And we'd love it if you helped us. Then, if we find anything, you can help us figure out what to do."

Mr. Jones looked at his wife. She smiled and said, "Tom, it'll be fine. We'll be there to keep an eye on the girls."

"Come on, Dad," pleaded Robin. "Say yes."

"Please, Tom," added Nezzie.

"OK," said Mr. Jones, "I'll go along with your plan, but you have to follow instructions exactly."

"We will," Nezzie and Robin chorused.

"I assume that Tara Lynn is in on this plan of yours, too," said Mrs. Jones.

"Of course," said Nezzie. "We'll call her as soon as we get home."

"Make sure she asks for permission," said Mrs. Jones. "If it's OK, tell Tara Lynn to be at our house around 1:30. That'll give us time to get some lunch, then find scruffy clothes for our excursion."

She sent a mock frown toward Robin and Nezzie. "This is not how I planned to spend my Sunday afternoon!"

Chapter 7

In Search
of Clues

That afternoon, the group descended upon the dump site at Marin Marsh. They all wore long-sleeved shirts, jeans, heavy boots, and two pairs of latex gloves.

Mrs. Jones issued her instructions. She finished the list by saying, "Stay on the outer edges of the pile. I don't want you climbing up on it. Do you understand me?"

"Yes, Mama," said Nezzie. "Outer edges only." Robin and Tara Lynn nodded in agreement.

"And don't get careless just because you're wearing gloves," Mrs. Jones warned.

"We'll remember everything you told us, Mama Jill," said Robin. She recited the list: "Only pick up what you can see clearly. Use a shovel to dig in the muck. If we find anything strange, call you or Dad to deal with it. Change gloves every so often. Put anything we pick up into a trash bag. Stay off the pile of trash."

Her father smiled. "Sounds like you know what to do." He leaned on a long-handled shovel and said, "So let's start detecting."

They moved into action. Tara Lynn immediately went to look for the envelope she had spied on the first trip to the dump site. However, the wind and animals had been at work. Things weren't exactly as they had been.

Tara Lynn dug in the general area with her shovel. After a few minutes, she called out, "Hey! I found it. Or at least, I found something." She used the shovel to scrape away leaves and dirt. Then she lifted a soggy sheet of paper.

Robin and Nezzie came to look. "What does it say?" asked Nezzie.

"It says . . . " began Tara Lynn. Then she stared at the paper in dismay.

"You can't read it," said Robin. "The writing is all smeared."

"So much for that clue," said Tara Lynn. She started toward a trash bag.

"Wait!" cried Robin. "Don't throw it away. Maybe when the paper dries out, we'll be able to read it."

"Yeah," said Nezzie. "Take it to Mama. She's in charge of what we collect."

So Tara Lynn carried the paper over to Mrs. Jones.

"Our first piece of evidence," said Nezzie's mother. "It's too wet right now to be much good, so I'll put it in the sun to dry." She spread the paper on top of a garbage bag she had put on the ground, then weighted it down with a small rock.

"This stuff sure does stink," said Nezzie as she returned to her task. "I never knew garbage could smell so bad."

"Just take a couple of slow, deep breaths," said Robin with a grin.

"Yeah, yeah," muttered Nezzie. She dug some more.

A few minutes later, Robin straightened up from her digging, a muddy envelope between her gloved fingers. "Hey, guys, there's a lot of mail over here. And some of the envelopes are in one piece, like whoever opened them used a letter opener."

"Let's see," said Nezzie as she and Tara Lynn headed toward Robin.

"Look," said Robin, "this envelope is addressed to Supreme Painters, on South Street."

Supreme Painters
202 South Street
Fort Wayne IN

"A clue!" cried Nezzie. "Hey, everyone, Robin found a real clue. An envelope addressed to some painters."

"That explains some of the stuff I'm finding," said Mr. Jones as he came over to inspect the envelope. "Paint cans. Half-empty bottles of paint remover. Things you'd expect painters to use."

"I've noticed something else," said Mrs. Jones, who had joined the group. "Old shingles, tar paper, and junk like that. Looks like someone's done a roofing job."

"Let's keep looking for mail," suggested Robin. "Maybe we can find the name of a roofing company, too."

"Hey, here's something!" called Mr. Jones a few minutes later. He was holding up a can. "It's malathion." He shook the can and the soft swish of liquid could be heard. "There's still some in here."

"Mala what?" asked Nezzie.

"Malathion," said Mr. Jones. "It's a pesticide. People use it in gardens to kill insects." He dug around some more. "Here's another can, and the lid's not—"

His wife interrupted. "Tom, what are those cans floating in the reeds over there?" She pointed. "See? Close to the shoreline? Can you get them?"

He sloshed over, scooped up the two containers, and read the labels aloud. "Malathion." He shook his head. "This is bad, girls. Very bad. Malathion is a poison. If it's not used properly, it can be a disaster."

"I think it's already a disaster, Dad," said Robin. "I'll bet that's what killed the fish."

"You're probably right."

"People shouldn't be dumping stuff like that anywhere," commented Mrs. Jones. "It's hazardous waste and it needs to be disposed of properly."

"We'd better tell Uncle Bill," said Nezzie.

"That's a good idea," agreed Robin. "He can tell the people at the water lab. They can test for mala, malathion first." She struggled with the awkward word. "If they rule it out, well, it's out. But if it turns out to be what killed the fish, then . . . " She shrugged—there wasn't much more to say.

They worked for another hour before Mrs. Jones called a halt. "I think we have enough to go on. We need to take home what we have so we can look it over and try to figure out what it all means."

They quickly packed their evidence and went home. As soon as they got to the house, Mr. Jones called Bill Harris to fill him in. Meanwhile, the girls laid out the papers, which were now fairly dry.

"Let's sort everything into groups," suggested Robin.

"Yeah," said Tara Lynn. "We'll put everything that looks like it came from the same place into the same pile."

A few minutes later, Robin spoke. "You know," she said, "a lot of this stuff is from the same businesses."

"I noticed that, too," said Nezzie. "That paint company has a lot, and so does Design It Graphics, whatever that is, and some place called Windmere Roofing." She pointed to the address on an envelope she was just smoothing out.

"Yeah, here's something else from Windmere," said Tara Lynn. "Look, there's a picture of a roof right beside the company name."

"It's called a logo," said Robin.

"Whatever," said Tara Lynn crossly. "It's still a picture of a roof."

"What about all that pesticide stuff? That mala . . . malathion. Any idea where that came from?" asked Nezzie. She searched through the scraps of paper.

"Here's something," said Tara Lynn. "One of these letters has Pest Control in the letterhead, but the first part of the name is ripped off. And there's a bug with a circle around it and a line through it. What Robin would call a 'lo-go.'" She drew the word out, exaggerating the vowels.

"Wait a minute," said Robin. "I've seen that somewhere."

"Seen what?" asked Tara Lynn.

"Where?" asked Nezzie.

"That logo—that bug with a circle around it and a line through it. You know, like 'no bugs allowed'. Or those 'no smoking' signs. The ones with the lit cigarette in a circle and a big line through it."

"Now that you mention it, I have, too. But where?"

"TV?" said Tara Lynn. "Maybe a commercial?"

"Maybe," said Robin, "but I was thinking I saw it on a truck or a van." She wrinkled her forehead, sucked on her lower lip, and thought hard. "I remember! Just before we moved to the farm, I saw a van with a logo like that on our street.

"Now, how can we find the name of the company?" continued Robin thoughtfully. "We've got most of it. Pest Control. Something Pest Control."

"Let's look it up," suggested Nezzie. She hurried off, returning with a phone book. She flipped through until she reached the yellow pages.

Nezzie turned to the Ps, then ran her finger down the page. "Personal Watercraft, Personnel Consultants, Pest Control Services."

"Oh no," wailed Tara Lynn, "there are tons of different companies."

"And most of them have Pest Control in their name," added Nezzie.

"Only three show a logo, and none are the one we want," added Robin.

"I was so sure we'd find it," complained Nezzie. "Now what do we do?" She twirled a braid around one finger. "Let's try to find some of the other businesses."

They spent the next half hour thumbing through the phone book and writing down phone numbers.

"So how are our girl detectives doing?" asked a teasing voice. The trio looked up to see Mr. and Mrs. Jones standing in the doorway.

"Are you making progress?" asked Mrs. Jones.

"Some," said Nezzie and Tara Lynn at the same time.

"A little," said Robin.

"We don't know who did the dumping yet, but we've got our evidence all organized," said Nezzie. She looked at Robin and Tara Lynn, and they nodded for her to continue.

"Well, you already know most of this, but here goes," Nezzie said. "Most of the mail we found is from the same four businesses. Here's our list: Windmere Roofing, Supreme Painters, Design It Graphics, and some pest control company. We don't know which one yet."

"So one of them must be the culprit, don't you think?" asked Tara Lynn.

"Well . . . " began Mrs. Jones.

Robin jumped in. "No. Don't you see, Tara Lynn, it wouldn't make sense for four different companies to be dumping their trash in the same spot at the same time."

"But the trash is there," said Tara Lynn.

"Yeah, but I'll bet these companies paid someone else to haul it away," concluded Robin. "Don't you agree, Dad? Mama Jill?"

Before the adults could answer, Nezzie broke in. "You're right, Robin. And if we can find who they hired to do their hauling, we'll know who dumped the stuff in the marsh."

Mr. Jones looked at his wife in wonder. "They *are* Nancy Drews."

Mrs. Jones laughed. "I wouldn't go that far. They're just smart young women, which we already knew.

"On a more serious note," she continued, "what are you planning to do next?"

"I have an idea!" cried Tara Lynn. "We could call the companies and pretend to do a survey. You know, say we were working on a school project about landfills and ask them how they handled their trash. If they took care of it themselves or if they hired somebody else to do it."

"Right," added Nezzie. "Then, we could make a list of the places that do the hauling and call them and—"

"Hold it right there," said Mr. Jones.

"Dad!" cried Robin.

Tom Jones looked at his wife for support. She thought for a moment, then said, "Well, you *are* working on a school project. This all came out of that food chain assignment, so that much is true.

"And I don't see any harm in contacting the businesses with the survey idea. You'll probably get a secretary or receptionist on the phone, so that's innocent enough. But . . ."

Mr. Jones took over. "Under no circumstances are you going to call any hauling companies. Whoever is doing the dumping is breaking the law and knows it. I won't have you dealing with criminals. You could put yourselves in danger."

"Dad, we—" began Robin.

He cut her off. "There is no discussion, Robin. Bill's people can handle it from that point." He paused and looked meaningfully at all three of the girls. "If we can't trust you not to approach the hauling companies, the project stops right here, right now!"

"Dad," said Robin, "we promise. Once we find out who the dumpers are, we'll tell you and Mama Jill. Then you guys can decide what to do."

"We'll be careful," Tara Lynn assured him. "We'll only call the businesses we told you about, and a few others that had mail in the trash heap. OK?"

"OK," said Tom.

"Don't forget, it's Sunday. Most places will be closed," added Mrs. Jones. "You probably won't have any luck until Tuesday."

"Well, we still want to start today," said Robin.

"Fine. But keep us posted," said her father. The adults left the girls clustered around the telephone.

"Where should we start?" asked Tara Lynn.

"Let's go in alphabetical order," suggested Robin. "So Design It Graphics would be first."

"Sounds good," said Nezzie. She picked up the phone and dialed the number. She listened intently, then hung

up. "I got an answering machine," she reported. "It says they're closed for the holiday. Call back on Tuesday."

They tried two more numbers with the same results.

"Nobody's working," complained Robin when her father stopped in to check on their progress. "Mama Jill was right. Everything's closed until Tuesday."

"Well, then, you'll just have to wait," said Mr. Jones. "If they're not open, they're not open. Why not put off all your calling until Tuesday?"

"But, Dad," said Robin, "we've got more businesses on the list. Maybe . . . "

"Robin," said Mr. Jones, "it's Sunday evening. Nothing is going to be open. Give it a rest."

The girls looked hopelessly at one another, then nodded. "All right," Nezzie grumbled.

Later, they sprawled on the floor in Robin's room.

"I just hate sitting here doing nothing," said Tara Lynn. "What if tonight's the night those creeps decide to dump another load of garbage in the marsh?"

"Yeah! I think we should have another stakeout," said Nezzie. "We could keep watch like we did last night."

"All we ended up with last night was a raccoon in the tent and a hole in Tara Lynn's backpack," said Robin.

"That was then, this is now. Are you in?" asked Nezzie.

The three girls looked at each other.

"I'm in," said Tara Lynn.

"Me, too," said Robin.

"Great," said Nezzie. "Now all we have to do is talk our folks into letting us camp out again tonight."

Chapter 8

More Detecting

"Dad was really surprised that I wanted to go camping again tonight," said Robin. She spread her sleeping bag across the floor of the tent. The girls had set up camp in the same spot as they had the night before.

Nezzie chuckled. "Mama was surprised, too. She said you must have really enjoyed yourself to want to go again so soon."

"I hope they don't suspect we're up to something," said Tara Lynn. "I thought your mother gave us kind of a funny look, Nezzie."

"Well, we didn't lie," said Nezzie defensively. "We said we wanted to camp out again. They didn't ask us where."

"But you know they think we're in the meadow," commented Robin.

"Yeah," admitted Nezzie. "And they'll have a fit if they find out we're not. I don't feel good about this, Robin, but they never would have given us permission to camp here. You know that."

"Well, look at it this way," said Robin slowly, "it's for a good cause. We're trying to catch the people spoiling our marsh. We're not—"

"*Our* marsh," teased Nezzie. "Listen to you."

Robin grinned. "Hey, I admit it. I like the butterflies and the wildflowers. And that crane we saw this afternoon—it was just gorgeous."

"That wasn't a crane," said Tara Lynn. "It was a blue heron. They are pretty, aren't they?"

"Oh yes," agreed Robin. "When it lifted its wings and flew off . . . " she sighed with pleasure. "It was just about the most beautiful thing I've ever seen."

Tara Lynn yawned, then stretched out on her sleeping bag.

"Don't you dare go to sleep," said Nezzie.

"I'm not," said Tara Lynn. "I'm just getting comfortable."

"Don't get too comfortable," said Robin. "We said we were going to stay up all night and keep watch."

"We are. We will. But do we all have to be awake at the same time? I'm still sleepy from last night." Tara Lynn yawned again. "I didn't realize how tired I was until we got here. As long as we were busy trying to solve this mystery, I was fine. Now that we're all quiet and cozy . . . " she yawned again. "I think last night's catching up with me."

"Shhh! Did you hear something?" asked Nezzie suddenly. She sat up and strained to listen. However, there was nothing to be heard but the swish of grass blowing against the side of the tent.

Tara Lynn looked over at Smitty, who was lying peacefully just outside the door of the tent. "If there was something out there, Smitty would have let us know."

"I guess you're right," said Nezzie. She lay back down.

Once again, the girls talked long into the night. Robin struggled to keep her eyes open as Tara Lynn told a long story about one of her brothers and his messy bedroom.

The next thing she knew, light filled the tent. They had fallen asleep—again.

"Nezzie! Tara Lynn!" called Robin. "Wake up!"

Nezzie rolled out of her sleeping bag. "Some detectives we are," she grumbled. "I can't believe we didn't stay awake."

Robin sighed. "I can. We haven't had a lot of sleep this weekend. And think about all the digging we did yesterday. It's no wonder we were tired."

"Do you suppose real detectives fall asleep on the job?" asked Tara Lynn.

"Probably," laughed Robin.

A short time later, they had taken down the tent and were headed to the house. "Today's Labor Day," commented Robin.

"I know," said Nezzie. "We'll have to help Mama get things ready for the cookout."

"What's there to do?"

Tara Lynn laughed. "You obviously haven't spent a holiday with Mrs. J. before. She cooks up a storm."

"That she does," said Nezzie. "And remember, we've got lots of company coming. Unless we have a house full of people, Mama doesn't think we've celebrated properly. And guess who her helpers are?"

"Us!" laughed Robin. "I don't mind, Nez. We never did much on holidays," she added quietly. "Mama usually had to work. And if she did have a day off, she just wanted some peace and quiet."

"Well, those are two things you won't find at this house—at least not on a holiday," said Nezzie.

Then she turned to Tara Lynn. "I know you have to hurry home this morning, but do you want to get together again tonight? Do you think we should try another stakeout?"

"I don't know," said Tara Lynn. "I doubt that Mom would let me. Three nights in a row might be pushing it."

"We've got school tomorrow," said Robin. "I don't think Dad or Mama Jill would go for it either."

They had reached the Jones's driveway. "I'll call you later," said Tara Lynn. "We can talk about it then." She waved good-bye and took off down the road toward her own house.

The rest of the day passed quickly. Robin enjoyed every minute of the Labor Day celebration. She had never seen so much food prepared in one kitchen before. Nor had she done so much to help fix it. But she certainly enjoyed the eating part.

One of the visiting families had a little girl who was less than a year old. Robin and Nezzie spent a lot of time playing with her and making her giggle. Then the four boys who were guests challenged them to a game of touch football. Before long, most of the adults joined in.

After football, it was time for a volleyball match. And when that was done, there was more eating to do.

At last the visitors left, calling out their thanks as they got into their cars. Robin stood in the driveway and waved until her arm was tired. It had been so much fun.

By six o'clock, she and Nezzie were done helping with cleanup. They went up to Nezzie's room to call Tara Lynn.

Robin dialed the number. "Are you coming over?" she asked as soon as Tara Lynn answered.

"No, I can't. Mom said I was wearing out my welcome."

Robin laughed, then said to Nezzie, "She can't come." She went back to her phone conversation. "Well, can you come over tomorrow after school? We want to try to make some of those phone calls."

"I'll ask if I can get off the bus with you guys," promised Tara Lynn. "I'm sure she'll let me." She paused, then added, "Too bad we still don't know about that pest control business. If we could find out who they are, it would be a really good lead."

"Yeah, it would," said Robin.

"Hey, Robin, what are you guys talking about?" asked Nezzie.

"Sorry, Nez," said Robin. "Here, come and listen in." She held the receiver so Nezzie could hear, too.

"Hi, Nezzie," said Tara Lynn. "I was just saying that it would be nice if we could find out who those pest people are."

"Hey, I just had an idea," exclaimed Robin. "What about the Internet?"

"What about it?" asked Tara Lynn.

But Nezzie had caught on. "Maybe they've got a Web site," she said excitedly. "Why didn't we think of that before? Tara Lynn, we'll call you back."

"I'll check things out on this end," said Tara Lynn. "If you guys find something before I do, call me right away."

Nezzie and Robin raced downstairs and poked their heads into the family room. "Mama," said Nezzie, "may we use the computer for a while? We need to check something out on the Internet."

Mrs. Jones glanced up from her book. "What are you looking for?"

"Pest control companies. Remember? It's one of our leads," said Nezzie.

Mr. Jones put down the magazine he was reading. "What's wrong with the phone book? If it's a local company, it'll be in there."

"We tried that, Dad," said Robin. "There must be 25 companies listed with 'pest control' in their names. Besides, we're looking for a logo. We thought it might be on a Web site even if it isn't in the phone book."

"Oh! Good idea," her father said.

"Go to it," added Mrs. Jones. "The computer is yours."

As the girls entered Mrs. Jones's small office, Robin said, "Let me do this. I'm a little quicker at it than you are."

"OK," said Nezzie. She dragged a chair over and sat close to Robin.

Robin punched a few keys on the keyboard. "Now, let's do a search for 'pest control,'" she said. She typed in the topic and a moment later read the results. "Oh no! There are 893 related entries!"

"That's too many hits!" exclaimed Nezzie.

"I just need to narrow the search," said Robin. She entered "pest control" and "Fort Wayne, Indiana". The machine hummed; then a much narrower selection of entries popped up.

"There are still over a hundred," complained Nezzie.

They scrolled down the list. "All we really need to do is check the ones that are companies or businesses. We can skip things like *Pesticide Use in Franke Park*," said Robin.

She clicked on A.J.'s Unlucky Bug Pest Control. The company's home page appeared—and it had a logo.

"A dead bug with a flower on its chest—wrong," sighed Nezzie.

Robin tried another company name. And another. Each time, the logos weren't right.

Twenty names later, Robin clicked on Duncan's Pest Control. The Web site popped up. "This is it!" she yelled. "Look at that logo!"

There on the screen was a big fat bug in a circle with a line through it.

Chapter 9

Grounded

"I thought school would never end," said Nezzie. She turned sideways in the seat so she could talk to Robin and Tara Lynn. The bus was noisy; she had to almost shout.

"I know what you mean," sighed Robin. "The worst part was when Mrs. Knox asked about how far we had gotten on our project. There wasn't much we could say because we haven't done much."

"I know," said Tara Lynn. "We got sidetracked by this fish kill business."

"We'd better put something on paper or we're gonna be in a world of trouble," commented Nezzie.

"We could start tonight," suggested Tara Lynn. "I have some information off the Internet that ought to help."

"And Robin and I got some books from the library," said Nezzie. "Maybe we can do an outline or something."

The bus lurched around a corner. "Hey, it's Tuesday!" said Robin.

"No kidding," said Nezzie. "It's been Tuesday all day."

"I'm serious," protested Robin. "Uncle Bill was going to take the water samples to the lab today, and Sarah probably worked on the fish again."

"That's right," said Tara Lynn. "I was so busy thinking about who we were gonna call, I forgot about the samples we collected."

"Yeah, but the water testing will take a few days to do," Nezzie said. "We might find out more just by making our phone calls."

The bus squeaked to a halt at Goose Haven Farm. When the girls ran into the house, calling out their hellos, they found Mrs. Jones in the kitchen making jelly.

"Hi, girls," she said. "How was your day?"

"Fine," said Nezzie. The other two nodded in agreement.

"If you guys can wait a minute, I'll fix something for a snack," Nezzie's mother said, pouring steaming liquid into a jar.

"That's OK, we're gonna make our phone calls now," said Robin.

"Oh, that's right," said Mrs. Jones. "Shout if you need me."

"We will," said Nezzie. She led the way to her mother's office.

"Let's try this one first," suggested Robin, pointing to a name on their list. She read off the number and Tara Lynn dialed.

"No answer."

"OK, try this one." Nezzie read another number.

This time, a woman answered. Tara Lynn explained why she was calling, then stopped abruptly. "She hung up on me! Boy, what a grump!"

"Why would she do that?" asked Nezzie.

"She said she didn't have time to be bothered with kids making crank calls." Tara Lynn rolled her eyes.

"Don't worry about her," said Robin. "Just try somebody else."

This time Tara Lynn got an answering machine. She hung up without leaving a message. "I'm not having much luck," she said. "Here, Nezzie, you try."

Nezzie took the phone. "Let's try Duncan's Pest Control," she suggested.

"Hello?" Nezzie covered the phone and whispered quickly, "I've got someone!" She spoke into the phone again. "Yes. This is Inez Anderson, and I'm calling about your waste management service. I . . . " She stopped and whispered to the others, "A kid answered. He went to get his mother."

Nezzie started again, "My name is Inez Anderson, and I'm working on a school science project about waste management and landfills." She paused briefly, then said, "Louis Middle School. Uh, it's Mrs. Knox.

"OK. Thank you. I just have two quick questions. Do you take care of your own waste removal or does someone do that for you? Yes, for your business." Nezzie hastily scribbled down an answer. "Thank you," she said. "Now my last question is this: do you know where they take your trash? The landfill? OK." She scribbled another note. "Thank you, Mrs. Duncan. I appreciate your help. Yes, I'll be sure to tell Mrs. Knox hello."

Nezzie hung up the phone. "She knows Mrs. Knox!"

"So what?" said Robin. "We *are* working on a science project. Sort of. Anyway, what did she say?"

"She said some outfit called Acme Hauling and Waste Removal takes their trash to the landfill."

"This is the best clue so far," said Tara Lynn. "We may have our culprit! Let me make the next call."

Tara Lynn dialed the number for Supreme Painters. "Hello? Supreme Painters?" She listened briefly, then continued. "Yes. Well, my name is Tara Lynn Meyers. I'm working on a school science project. May I ask you a few questions?

"Yes. I need to contact four companies and ask about their waste management policies. Yes. We're talking about pollution and the environment in science class. Yes. Oh, really? That's nice." She rolled her eyes. "So, do you take care of your own trash or do you hire somebody to do it for you?

"I see. Do you know where they take it?" She made circles on her notepad. "The landfill, of course. Yes, sir. Yes, sir. Thank you. Oh! Really? That's nice. Well, thank you. No, sir. That's it. Thank you very much."

She plunked the phone down. "I thought I'd never get off. He wanted to talk and talk and talk."

"Well, you complained about the woman who *didn't* want to talk to you," laughed Robin.

"Anyway," said Tara Lynn, "get this. It's Acme Hauling and Waste Removal again. According to the guy at Supreme Painters, their trash goes to the landfill. He even talked about the hazardous waste a painting company has. He says Acme takes special care of that stuff."

"Yeah, I'll bet they do," muttered Robin.

"This is the second time Acme Hauling's name has come up," said Nezzie. "Both of those places we've talked to are small businesses. And they both use Acme. It seems kind of suspicious to me."

"You know what our folks would say about jumping to conclusions," warned Robin. "I think we're on the right track, but let's call a couple more places."

The girls took turns dialing numbers. Two calls never picked up. Several numbers reached answering machines.

Then Nezzie called Windmere Roofing. Robin and Tara Lynn listened as she asked the usual questions.

"Bingo!" cried Nezzie as she replaced the receiver. "Another small company. Another contract with Acme!"

"Obviously, Acme is dumping the stuff in the marsh," said Robin.

"I think you're right," agreed Nezzie. "These businesses are all different. The only thing they have in common, besides being small, is that they hired Acme to haul their trash. And we found some of that trash in Marin Marsh. It's elementary, my dear Watson."

"We're supposed to be Nancy Drew, not Sherlock Holmes," said Robin.

"Whatever."

"Let's tell Mama Jill and Dad what we've found out," suggested Robin.

Mr. and Mrs. Jones were in the family room when the girls burst in with their news. "We think we know who's doing the illegal dumping," announced Nezzie. She strutted across the floor and stood in front of her mother and Tom.

"And who might that be?" Mr. Jones asked.

"Acme Hauling and Waste Removal," said Robin.

"We called a bunch of companies on our list," said Tara Lynn. "Most of the ones we talked to use Acme."

"And Acme isn't taking it where they say they are," said Nezzie, "because everyone thinks it's going to the landfill."

"That's a strong accusation," said Mrs. Jones. "Acme can get into a lot of trouble if what you say is true. Are you sure?"

"We're sure, Mama," said Nezzie. She held out the notebook and showed her mother the notes from their phone calls.

"I think they've got pretty good evidence against this company, Tom," said Mrs. Jones.

"Perhaps. But there will have to be some real proof before anyone can accuse Acme. I'll call Bill and let him know what you found out. Then he can get the authorities involved." Mr. Jones reached for the phone and started to dial.

The girls listened anxiously. "Tomorrow?" he asked, after explaining what the girls had discovered. "We'll have it ready. Yeah, yeah, OK." He hung up.

"What'd he say?" asked Robin.

"Oh, he said thank you," said her father, picking up his newspaper.

"Dad," said Robin, annoyed, "stop teasing. What did he say?"

"He said that you were great detectives and he thought you had some good evidence against Acme Hauling."

"Yes!" yelled Robin and Nezzie.

"I knew it," said Tara Lynn. "I knew we had 'em cold."

"And," continued Mr. Jones, "he said he'd stop by tomorrow to pick up your notes. He's going to turn them over to the authorities and let them take it from here." He grinned. "They'll have The Case of Illegal Dumping at Marin Marsh wrapped up in no time."

"They will?" asked Robin.

"But what about us?" asked Tara Lynn.

"You girls have done a great job," said Mrs. Jones.

"I can't believe how much you've found out in such a short time. You should be proud of yourselves."

"So, that's it?" said Robin. "That's all?"

"What else do you want?" asked Mrs. Jones in a puzzled voice.

"We want to catch 'em in the act," said Robin. "Like Nancy Drew."

Mrs. Jones chuckled. "So, what would Nancy do in a situation like this?"

"Jill," said Mr. Jones, "Don't encourage them! The next thing you know, they'll be wanting to stake out the dump site and catch the bad guys on videotape or something like that." He shook his head.

"Dad," said Robin, "that's a great idea."

Tara Lynn and Nezzie looked at one another. "The video camera," said Tara Lynn.

90

"Why didn't we think of that the last time?"

"Hey," said Mr. Jones, "I was just making a comment. I was not suggesting—"

"Excuse me?" said Mrs. Jones. "What last time?"

"Ooops," said Tara Lynn, covering her mouth with both hands.

"Tara Lynn? What did you mean?" said Mrs. Jones.

"Oh, she was just . . . " began Nezzie.

"We . . . " Robin trailed off, not sure what to say.

Mr. Jones looked from his wife's angry face to the girls' distressed ones. "Am I missing something?"

"I don't know, but I'm going to find out," said Mrs. Jones. She looked sternly at her daughter. "Inez Denise Anderson, I don't want any foolishness. Tell me exactly what Tara Lynn is talking about. What last time?"

Suddenly, all three girls were talking at once. They tried to explain about the camping trips. That they knew they were supposed to stay in the meadow. That somehow they had gotten the idea about watching the dump site and ended up in the marsh. They even shared details about the raccoon stealing their food and Smitty chasing it up a tree.

Mr. Jones frowned. "I can't believe you girls did this! We trusted you!"

"Nezzie," said her mother, "I am truly disappointed in you. How could you disobey me this way?"

Nezzie hung her head in shame.

"And you, too." Mrs. Jones turned to Robin and Tara Lynn. "All three of you knew where we expected you to be. What if something had happened? No one would have been there to help you."

"Nothing happened, Mrs. J. We just—" began Tara Lynn.

"Don't even try to make excuses," said Mrs. Jones. "You're just lucky that nothing happened." She glared at Nezzie and Robin. "The two of you are grounded until further notice. That means no telephone, no CD players, no whatever else I can come up with."

Then she directed her glare at Tara Lynn. "I'll be calling your mother tonight. I'm sure you'll get the same punishment once she finds out what happened."

"But, Mama," began Nezzie.

"End of discussion," said Mrs. Jones. "I'm too upset to talk right now. Go upstairs."

"But, Mama Jill," pleaded Robin.

Her father broke in. "Not another word from any of you. Robin and Nezzie—upstairs. Tara Lynn—you had better head home."

"You and your big mouth," muttered Nezzie as the three girls left the room.

"I'm sorry," said Tara Lynn. "It just sort of slipped out."

"Yeah, and now we're 'just sort of' grounded," grumbled Robin.

Chapter 10

Unexpected Help

When they got home from school on Wednesday, Robin and Nezzie went straight to Mrs. Jones's office to use the computer. Time was running out. Their science report was due in two days.

"We've got to get the outline and rough draft done tonight," said Robin.

"Too bad Tara Lynn isn't here," commented Nezzie. "She has a lot of stuff we need."

"We could e-mail her," suggested Robin.

"OK," said Nezzie. "I guess that's the best we can do. Report or no report, Mama isn't going to forget that we're grounded."

They got to work, looking over the information they had collected at the library and by observing the marsh. "One thing I want in our report is something about how the food chain is balanced," said Nezzie. "I want to show that what people do can throw things out of whack."

"I like that idea," said Robin. "I hadn't really thought much about that before. I just figured everything was the way it's supposed to be and it would stay that way." She erased a misspelled word on the paper in front of her. "I mean, I was careful not to litter and stuff like that, but I never thought much about what might be in the trash and how it might affect the food chain." She paused, then added, "I guess this project has made me look at things differently."

As soon as the girls finished going through their notes, they e-mailed Tara Lynn. She answered, adding her own complaints about being grounded. She also sent the information she had collected.

The girls e-mailed back and forth for several hours— working on an outline, then a rough draft. At last they were done.

"Wow, I can't believe we got this much done," said Nezzie. "You're a great writer, Robin."

They watched as the printer spit out the pages. "Let's have Mama take a look at this," Nezzie added. "I always have her read my reports before I turn them in. She's pretty good at spotting mistakes or things I've left out. That's one good thing about having a writer in the family."

"Will she fix stuff for us?" asked Robin.

"No way," said Nezzie. "She'll just kind of point out that a paragraph needs attention, or she'll ask enough questions to let us know that something is missing."

The girls found Mrs. Jones in the kitchen. She had notes and books spread out all over the table.

"Mama," said Nezzie, "would you look at this for us? It's our report on the food chain."

Mrs. Jones took off her glasses and rubbed her eyes. "Sure. I need a break from my work anyway." She shoved aside her notes, settled back in the chair, and began to read, making comments and asking questions as she made her way through the report.

"Very interesting," said Mrs. Jones when she finished. She looked at the girls thoughtfully. "You make some excellent points about how every one of us has a responsibility to the environment. I also like the part where you say the wetlands is an important ecological system. You girls have put a lot of work—and a lot of thought—into this project."

"Thanks, Mama Jill," said Robin.

"Yeah, thanks, Mom," added Nezzie.

"I'd like to see this again after you finish," said Mrs. Jones.

"Sure thing, Mom," said Nezzie. The girls hurried off to make the changes Mrs. Jones had suggested. Then they sent the finished report to Tara Lynn for her comments. By dinnertime, their final copy was printed out and ready to hand in. Nezzie took a second copy to her mother.

Later, at the dinner table, Mrs. Jones glanced at her husband. He nodded, then said, "We'd like to talk to you, girls."

"Yes," added Mrs. Jones. "I showed Tom your report.

And we—well, we think that we should help you guys solve this mystery."

"What!" exclaimed Robin.

"You mean—" began Nezzie.

"Don't get the wrong idea," interrupted her mother. "The pair of you are still grounded. That hasn't changed. You deserve that as punishment for lying. However," she added, "after reading your report, we do understand your concern for the environment and your dedication to clearing up this mystery."

"I'm really surprised to see how passionate you've become, Robin," said her father. "I've never heard you say much about the environment before, but after Jill showed me your report, I can see that you've developed a real appreciation for it."

Robin and Nezzie nodded, wondering what was coming next.

"Because of that," said Mrs. Jones, "Tom and I have decided to camp out with you so we can help you stake out the dump site—" She was interrupted by cheers from Robin and Nezzie.

"Can we call Tara Lynn and tell her?" asked Nezzie when she calmed down.

"No. You can't use the phone, remember? I'll call her mother and ask. Tom and I thought we might try a stake-out tonight and over the next few days. Wednesday and Thursday are trash collection days in the business section of town, so there's a good chance—"

Nezzie threw her arms around her mother. "Oh, Mama, thank you."

"Thank you, Dad," said Robin, kissing his cheek. "And let's take the video camera. That way, if anyone shows up, we can catch them on tape."

"Where do you suggest that we set up camp?" asked Mrs. Jones.

"In the grove of trees where Tara Lynn and I found those arrowheads," said Nezzie.

"That's a good spot," said Mrs. Jones. "But is it close enough to videotape anything?"

"Sure," said Robin. "The camera has a zoom lens. That'll bring whoever's there up close."

Her father shook his head. "Stakeouts. Video cameras. I can't believe I agreed to go along with this scheme."

Robin grinned. "You're part of the team, Dad. Just another Nancy Drew."

Chapter 11

Caught in the Act

"Everybody ready for this stakeout?" called Mr. Jones as he hoisted the tent bag onto his shoulder.

"Yes!" chorused Robin, Nezzie, and Tara Lynn.

"Ready, willing, and able," added Mrs. Jones. "Except for Smitty, of course." They had agreed to leave the dog at home, since his barking would alert the dumpers.

"OK, let's go."

The three girls led the way as the group trooped down the driveway, across the meadow, and into the marsh. Everyone was loaded down with gear—sleeping bags, a small cooler, binoculars, the video camera, and food.

In a short time they reached the campsite. Soon the tent was up and everything was ready.

"Now, even though we're staking out the scene of the crime, we have to get some sleep," said Nezzie's mother. "We all have school or work tomorrow."

"So we'll take turns keeping an eye on the dump site,"

finished Robin's father. He held up his wrist. "Each person in turn gets to use my watch. It has an alarm we can set to signal the next shift."

Then he picked up the camera. "I got some special film," he said. "It'll pick stuff up in almost no light." He fiddled with the camera to make sure it was ready to go.

Soon darkness fell. Nezzie offered to take first watch, so everyone else zipped themselves into their sleeping bags. Nezzie took up a position outside with the binoculars focused on the dump site.

It took Robin some time to fall asleep. She kept thinking about the dumpers and what it would be like to actually catch them in the act. She wished that she could be the one to do it. She wished she could meet them face-to-face and tell them exactly what she thought of them. How could they let poisons loose in the marsh? Didn't they know how wrong it was? Didn't they realize that they were killing marsh creatures? Didn't they care?

It seemed like only a moment later that Tara Lynn was shaking Robin's shoulder. "Robin," she whispered, "it's your turn to watch now."

Robin struggled out of her sleeping bag and went outside. "Nothing going on?" she asked as she took the binoculars and her father's watch from Tara Lynn.

"Not a thing," yawned Tara Lynn. "Good luck. I'm going to try to get some sleep now."

Robin sat at the edge of the campsite, staring intently at the distant pile of trash. The night wrapped itself around her like a fluffy blanket. She could hear the swish of the marsh grasses in the breeze. An owl's mournful hoot echoed over the water. The occasional plunk of a frog or fish in the water sounded like the drip of a leaky faucet.

Robin was almost nodding off when the alarm sounded. She stood up, stretched, and went to get her father, who had the next watch. Then she crawled back into her sleeping bag.

It was daylight when Robin opened her eyes again. For a moment, she had trouble remembering where she was. Then it came to her. She was on a stakeout in the marsh. And since it was morning, the stakeout had hardly been successful. She rolled over to find Nezzie wide awake as well.

"Nothing happened," said Nezzie glumly.

"So now what do we do?" whispered Robin.

Her father sat up and stretched. "We try again tonight," he said.

"Really?" exclaimed Nezzie. "You'll really do it again?"

"Absolutely," replied Mr. Jones. "Your mom and I said we wanted to help you solve this mystery, didn't we? Well, we haven't solved it yet. Our detective team will be on the job until we do."

Robin and Nezzie exchanged a smile. We really are a team, thought Robin. Nezzie and Tara Lynn and me. And Mama Jill and Dad, too.

Minutes later, they had wakened the still-sleeping Tara Lynn. The girls rolled up their sleeping bags, then joined Mrs. Jones outside, where she was keeping watch.

Robin gazed across the marsh toward the dump site. "What if they come during the day?" she asked.

"We'll have to take that chance," replied her father. "But I don't think they will, Robin. The dump site isn't that far from the road. They sure wouldn't risk dumping a load of trash when they might be spotted."

He began to dismantle the tent. "Time to get a move on, girls. We all have to get ready for school."

Half an hour later, they reached Goose Haven Farm. "I'll take you to school with me," Mr. Jones said. "That'll give you a few extra minutes. So get hopping. We leave at 8:30."

Robin, Nezzie, and Tara Lynn rushed upstairs to shower and dress. Back downstairs, they each had a quick bowl of cereal. Then they grabbed their backpacks and hurried outside to find Robin's father standing by the car, keys in hand.

"Did you remember our report?" asked Tara Lynn.

"I've got it," said Robin, patting her backpack.

"Yeah, we're actually a day early," added Nezzie with satisfaction.

"It's a good thing we finished last night," said Tara Lynn. "I'm too excited about our stakeout to think about writing a report today."

"Yeah, but we still have to think about the oral part of this assignment," sighed Robin. "I'm dreading that."

"Come on, Robin," said Nezzie. "You did most of the writing on this report. You'll do fine on the oral presentation."

"Yeah," added Tara Lynn. "This is the best report I've ever had my name on. And it's 'cause of you."

Robin looked from Nezzie to Tara Lynn. "Do you mean that?"

"Absolutely," said Nezzie. "You may not have liked the idea of studying the marsh at first, Robin, but you really got into it."

"Let's just be sure we get to work together the next time we have to do a project," said Tara Lynn.

Robin sank back into the seat, a feeling of satisfaction washing over her. Even if she completely flubbed the oral presentation, she didn't care. Not if Nezzie and Tara Lynn actually wanted her to work with them again. Not if they were her friends.

That night, they set up camp in the same spot. Again they took turns keeping watch. And again, nothing happened.

When she woke, Robin felt like crying. Without proof, they would never be able to pin the dumping on

Acme. And unless they did that, it might not stop. At least not before even more damage had been done to the marsh.

"Are we going to have to give up?" she asked her father as he took down the tent one more time. "You said they'd probably dump on Wednesday or Thursday night. But they didn't."

"Well, maybe I was wrong about that," said Mr. Jones.

His wife chimed in. "We're not giving up yet, Robin. Maybe they don't dump on the same day they pick up the trash."

"You mean we're going to try again tonight?" asked Nezzie in excitement.

Mrs. Jones yawned. "Yes, I guess that's what we mean," she said. "Though it's getting harder every night to stay awake."

An hour later, the girls were in school. Robin realized that she had been so busy that she hadn't even worried about her oral report. And now the day had arrived.

All morning, she watched the clock creep along toward 1:00, when it was time for science class. At lunchtime, she could hardly eat. She sat at the table, reading her notes over and over.

Then it was time. The written reports were handed in. The oral presentations started. Nezzie was one of the first, since they went alphabetically. Robin was scheduled for close to the end of the period, when they hit the Js.

She wished she was a Z so she wouldn't have to go until Monday or Tuesday.

"Robin, you're next," said Mrs. Knox.

Robin got to her feet. She shuffled through her notes, her heart thumping wildly. Then she looked at Nezzie and Tara Lynn. They both winked at her.

Robin stuck her notes into her jeans pocket and started to talk. At first her voice quavered, but it soon got stronger.

"When we got this assignment," she said, "I didn't want to study the marsh. I thought it was dirty and slimy and yucky. But now I know better. It's a carefully balanced ecological system. We can upset that balance if we're not careful. It's up to every one of us to make sure that doesn't happen. We're all responsible for keeping the environment clean and safe." She pointed at her classmates in turn. "And that includes you and you and you. And me," she concluded. "That's what I got from this project. And that's what I'm going to remember from now on."

She sat down before her legs collapsed under her. Nezzie started clapping. Soon everyone else in the class was, too.

Night three of the stakeout started just like nights one and two. Once again, Robin had the third watch. She was half-dozing and half-watching the dump site when she heard something. It was the low drone of a distant truck engine.

She grabbed the video camera in one hand and moved closer to the edge of the marsh, straining to hear better. The sound got louder and louder.

Robin dashed for the tent. "Someone's coming!" she hissed. "Wake up, you guys!" Then she dashed back to the edge of the campsite. Shivering with excitement, she focused the binoculars on the road that led to the trash heap. She could just make out the silhouette of a dump truck, backlit by the bright moonlight.

"What is it?" whispered her father.

Robin handed him the binoculars. "Look at the edge of the access road," she said. "There's a dump truck there."

They were soon joined by Mrs. Jones, Nezzie, and Tara Lynn.

"I want to see too!" complained Nezzie, rubbing the sleep from her eyes.

"Here, look through the binoculars," said Mr. Jones. He handed them to Nezzie.

"I can't read what it says on the truck," said Nezzie.

"It starts with *A*," said Robin. "It's Acme, I'm sure."

"Well, let's get our evidence," Mr. Jones suggested.

"Oh, yeah! I almost forgot," said Robin. She began to hand the video camera to her father.

"No, you do it, Robin," he said. "You're the one who spotted these guys. Now finish the job."

Robin's hands shook slightly as she lifted the camera to her eye. Through the lens, she followed the truck's progress down the access road. At the same time, Nezzie and Tara Lynn watched with the binoculars.

107

Robin started taping. First she took a wide-angle shot of the entire area so whoever watched the videotape would be able to tell where it was taped. Then she adjusted the zoom lens and focused on the truck. It pulled up to the edge of the marsh and stopped.

Robin zoomed in closer, trying to capture the man who got out of the passenger side of the truck. He had bushy eyebrows and a scraggly gray beard. An old baseball cap and faded overalls completed the picture. He waved his hand in a circular motion.

"What are you getting?" whispered her father.

"I can see them clearly," said Robin. "One man got out to direct the driver. He's telling him to back up. Now the rear of the truck is opening up and the garbage is being dumped." The camera made soft humming noises as it recorded the action.

"Great. Keep taping," said Mr. Jones. "I want to make sure we've got enough evidence to really nail these guys."

Robin taped the trash rolling out of the truck and onto the heap at the edge of the creek. She taped the bearded man scratching his head and talking to the driver. She taped the driver when he stuck his head out the window to say something to his partner. Then she focused on the truck itself. The black lettering of Acme Hauling and Refuse Removal stood out in sharp contrast against the grimy white background of the truck.

"How can they do this?" whispered Mrs. Jones to no one in particular. She, Tara Lynn, and Nezzie were watching the disgusting scene through their binoculars.

"I don't know," said Robin, "but they're going to be sorry. You can't mess up the environment like this. It's not right."

She kept on taping until the dumping was finished. The driver lowered the back of the truck. The bearded man got in. Then they pulled away, leaving one more pile of trash behind them.

"We've got 'em," said Robin as she turned off the camera. "We've got them on tape. And tape doesn't lie."

Chapter 12

In the News

"We should've heard something by now," said Nezzie. "It's been two whole weeks. All we know is that there definitely was malathion in the water. And that's definitely what poisoned the fish."

The three girls were sitting in the Jones's family room, talking and having an after-school snack.

"I know," said Tara Lynn. "Uncle Bill was really excited to get our videotape. I wonder why he hasn't called to let us know what's happening."

"Dad said these things take time," said Robin. "Even with the tape, the authorities have to check things out."

"There's no way Acme can weasel out of this!" exclaimed Nezzie. "We caught 'em red-handed." She pulled a bowl of popcorn closer and took a huge handful.

Robin picked up the remote control and turned on the television. "It feels so good not to be grounded. I never knew I'd miss the telephone and television so much."

Tara Lynn laughed. "Mom says we made up for it with e-mail."

"Yeah," said Robin as she absentmindedly flipped

through channels. "Dad said that if I'm grounded again, I won't get to use the computer, either. I guess that's because we tied up the phone line."

Suddenly Nezzie let out an excited yelp. "Robin! Back up! Back up! Go to Channel 25."

"Huh? Why?" asked Robin. "I'm looking for—"

"Forget it, whatever it is," said Nezzie. "Get to the news. I think I saw . . . "

Robin had reached Channel 25. And now they all saw what Nezzie had seen. There on the television screen was a bearded man directing an Acme dump truck.

"It's our tape," gasped Tara Lynn.

"Mama Jill, Dad!" yelled Robin. "Come here! Now!"

Mr. and Mrs. Jones ran into the room. "What's going on?" asked Mrs. Jones.

"Is there a problem?" asked Mr. Jones.

The girls pointed at the television.

"It's our tape," said Nezzie.

"On the news," said Robin, "they're showing our tape—"

"Shhh! I can't hear!" Nezzie snatched the remote control and turned up the volume.

A reporter was describing the scene. "What you see here is actual footage of the illegal dumping that's been going on at Marin Marsh. Acme Hauling and Refuse Removal has been indicted on several counts of environmental pollution."

"They've been caught!" shouted Robin.

"Hush," said her father. "Let's hear the rest of it."

The reporter continued, "Three local girls are credited with alerting the Department of Natural Resources to the illegal dumping. They also identified the culprits by going undercover and secretly taping the dumping. This is a copy of their videotape."

"Undercover!" hollered Nezzie. "We're real detectives!"

"I gotta call home," said Tara Lynn. She scrambled for the phone.

"Hey look, girls. There's Sarah," said Mrs. Jones.

Sarah Rosario appeared on the screen. She was standing on the beach at Hominy Ridge Lake. The camera also caught the dead fish that littered the beach.

"Part of the problem," Sarah was explaining to her interviewer, "is that some of the refuse that was dumped into the marsh contained a pesticide called malathion. There were a few other chemicals found in significant concentrations, but malathion was the big one. That's what killed all these fish. And," she paused for emphasis, "it's going to take some time get the water back to normal."

The camera panned the shoreline, showing more dead fish. Then it moved to the reporter. "This is Jeanette Jordan, live at Hominy Ridge Lake in Marin Marsh. More on this story later."

The news anchor moved on to the weather. Nezzie turned the volume down. For a moment, it was silent in the family room. Then Robin jumped to her feet. "We did it! We got the bad guys!"

"We'll be famous!" added Tara Lynn.

The next day, the indictment of Acme Hauling was front-page news in the *Fort Wayne News Journal*.

Robin read every word of the article. "It says that if Acme is convicted, they have to pay for the cleanup, *and* they'll get fined, *and* some company officials could even go to jail," she reported.

"Yeah, and that's not all," said Nezzie, who was looking through another section of the paper. "Listen to this!" She started to read:

"Three students from Louis Middle School, Inez Anderson, Robin Jones, and Tara Lynn Meyers, were instrumental in breaking up the illegal dumping operation. 'The city of Fort Wayne is fortunate to have such responsible young people living in our community,' said Mayor Ivan Worth. 'I will be contacting them and their parents to issue an invitation to next month's Community Service Awards banquet. They have earned this honor for their hard work and dedication to the environment.'"

"An award!" shouted Nezzie. "Hot dog! Wait until Tara Lynn and Mrs. Knox and all the kids at school hear. This is even better than the A we got on our project. It's the best thing that's happened all year!"

Robin looked from Nezzie's beaming face to Mama Jill's wide grin to her father's proud smile. "An award is pretty cool," she said, "but it's not the best thing that's happened. Getting to be part of an awesome family of detectives—that's the best."

The smiles got even bigger. And Robin's was the biggest of all.